Identity Papers

a novel by Anthony Cronin

Co-op
books
Dublin

First published in 1979 by Co-op Books Publishing Ltd,
50 Merrion Square, Dublin 2, Ireland.
Copyright © Anthony Cronin 1979

ISBN 0 905441 23 0

Cover Design: John Devlin

*Co-op Books Publishing Ltd and the Irish Writers' Co-operative exist to provide
outlets for new Irish fiction through publications and the organisation of public
readings.*

Co-op Books Publishing Ltd acknowledges the assistance of An Chomhairle Ealaion
in the publication of this book. The author would also like to acknowledge their
assistance by way of a grant in its completion.

Printed in Ireland by the Appletree Press
7 James Street South
Belfast BT2 8DL

For Francis Stuart,
this ...?

Author's Note
This is a work of fiction; and all the characters and events
described in it are the products of the author's imagination.
The events are, however, supposed to take place some time in
the summer of 1966; and the date is of some significance where
what might be called the psycho-sexual preoccupations and
attitudes of the characters are concerned.

"... On the surface layer of his personality the average man is reserved, polite, compassionate, responsible, conscientious. There would be no social tragedy of the human animal if this surface layer of the personality were in contact with the deep natural core. This, unfortunately, is not the case. The surface layer of social co-operation is not in contact with the deep biologic core of one's selfhood; it is borne by a second, an intermediate character layer, which consists exclusively of cruel, sadistic, lascivious, rapacious and envious impulses ... . If one penetrates through this second layer of perversion ... one always discovers the third, deepest layer which we call the biologic core. In this core, under favourable social conditions, man is an essentially honest, industrious, co-operative, loving, and, if motivated, rationally hating animal. Yet ... drop this mask of cultivation and it is not natural sociality that prevails at first, but only the perverse, sadistic character layer.*

Wilhelm Reich,
"The Mass Psychology of Fascism"

"The first duty of a gentleman is to keep himself out of the hands of the police."

Villiers De l'Isle Adam,
Cruel Stories

Book 1

*H*e awoke. He became conscious of a dim, oblong area of light in surrounding darkness. And of a phrase also, used recently in dream or life: "Surrender myself to the law." He became aware also that he had slept in his clothes.

He remembered. The words belonged to the rhetoric of the night before and had been used in drunken bravado to mock the sordid reality he had to face this morning, if it was morning. He had in fact to surrender himself to the law. He had to go to court. And he was in Jonathen Edwards' studio where there was no clock and where he, having no watch and being unfamiliar with the morning sounds, had no means of telling the time.

What time was it? Was it day? Had he "slept it out"?

He lay on his side, apparently turned towards the large window, but he did not know whether the grey effulgence he saw was the effect of the dawn, of daylight on a dark morning, or of a street lamp in the alleyway. It looked like the light of a murky dawn to him, but then he did not know how translucent the curtains might be. For all he knew it was broad daylight and the hunt was up for him on the head of his having failed to appear in the dock and stand his trial like a man as he had sworn to do.

Had he sworn? He could not remember. It seemed likely that he had.

The dead heat of his socks, the rough itch of trousers at knees and ankles, the sweaty clasp of his shirt at neck and wrists made him bitterly regret having flopped in like this on the night before an occasion when it was necessary to appear at his most presentable, however little presentable that was nowadays. He decided accordingly to remove his clothes. Whether or no the damage was done and even if he had to put them on again almost immediately he would assuage the guilt by taking off the clothes. That was the way to treat guilt.

He doubled his legs up towards him and tugged first one sock and then the other back and downwards with the hook of his right thumb. This eased and cooled his feet but the effort wakened him fully and brought besides the knowledge that his general physical condition was not, at the moment, tip top. He pushed the socks towards the end of the bed with his feet to eject them and discovered that the blankets had edged up and sideways so that when his legs were stretched out fully his feet were uncovered to the air. He let them project into the gentle element for a while. It was the first pleasant sensation of the new day, if it was day. Then his feet began to get unpleasantly cold. He brought his knees up, but, after a while, he had, naturally, an acute desire to stretch, both mental and physical. It manifested itself physically as an actual pain, a sort of ache behind the knee joints. He decided to let his feet project and to keep the rest of his clothes on for the moment at least; that he could do no more, whatever the moral or physical imperatives, for the moment at least.

As soon as he was again inactive he became again concerned about the question of the time. Listening intently for a clue he heard nothing except a sort of murmur that could well have been in his own ears, the mere noise of being alive. What time was dawn? The truth of the matter was that he did not know, except very vaguely, and then only by working on the notoriously inaccurate twelve hour system. It did not appear to be very bright outside, but that meant little for there were too many variables, including the opacity of the curtains and the state of the weather. He still could not hear anything except the aforesaid murmur, but that did not mean much either, for he could have woken during that curious housewife's lull in mid morning when the commuting traffic has passed on its inward journey, the radios go off and silence is restored to the more residential streets.

Now he thought he heard rain. Or was it traffic? A soft swishing sound that could be rain on a garden or distant cars on a wet surface. Lying quite still he worried acutely, heart thumping at the thought that it was all over and the next thing would be the police banging at the door with a bench warrant, whatever that might be.

Suddenly he heard a solitary bird go cheep cheep. It was a soft cry, but it seemed to carry, as through the dawn. Cowering, hoping and listening desperately, he heard others, several. Had the birds been singing unbeknownst to him since he woke? His hearing being occluded by his fears? Or had he just heard the first bird and the general awakening? He could now distinguish varieties of song—if song you choose to call it—high and low, presumably the utterance of big and small, but had they been at it all the time or not? He had no certainty whatever. It was even possible that he had awoken during a pause in the choirings, that it was broad day on a dark day and the birds were only at it now and then, to keep their pecker up. The birds in any case he knew started twice: sleepily, before dawn, and cruelly, after. One way or another the birds were not, to him at the moment, much of a guide.

He heard a clock strike or a bell sound and listened intently with an almost muscular motion of both ears, even lifting his head off the pillow to do so and enduring the penalty in pain, but after the first two or three strokes or soundings he heard nothing more except the faint peepings or cheepings of the birds.

Then in the distance he heard the hooves of a pony coming at a fast clip. His heart rose. He pulled what he could of the bedclothes about him, drew up his knees and felt for the first time almost secure. A frenzied driving of small ponies and deep-bottomed carts round the quieter streets and the lanes at the back of them was an indubitably morning activity in Dublin, and an early one at that. The pony passed, seemingly down the lane at the end of the garden, doubtless with a

11

corrugated drum of pig food in the cart affair and a boy standing up behind it whistling—as well he might, having life before him and probably as yet no troubles with the law.

The Baron decided that it was somewhere around seven o'clock in the morning.

Now that he had some little certainty that he could rest or skulk or cower where he was for an appreciable length of time he considered again taking off his trousers. The old tweeds of course, the last relics of old decency, stood any amount of battering, but there would be something symbolic about dressing to go to court later, when he got up, dressing for the sacrifice.

In the case of women, of course, it was undressing for the sacrifice.

With a series of convulsive movements he got the trousers off and pushed them out of the bed.Then he heard, faintly but unmistakably, the clop and scrape of the hooves of a heavier, more deliberate, wiser and more disciplined animal than the pony, followed by the musical clink of milk bottles. This was not too good, for, in the Baron's general experience, milk was seldom delivered before eight or half past eight in central Dublin. The pig boy was a lazy little bugger who would not go far in the pig food or any other business. Of course on the other hand milk might be delivered specially early in this area. It could be a fortunate one, specially favoured by a dairy king who was forever on the telephone to subordinates demanding early delivery in it to prove to someone or other that he had a lot of power and that he loved her. Susan. All in all, he decided, it was probably no more than about eight o'clock at worst. He could, and should, rest on a little more. He tried to take comfort from the fact that in about three hours from now he would be surrounded by the everyday therapeutics of a public house. He imagined the peace of an ideal snug: the racing page, a gin and Roses and quiet sunlight caressing an upper panel. His wish to believe that this particular morning's proceedings would be, at worst, inconclusive, and probably over before you knew you were there, was based on the assurances of those who ought to know; but in spite of what he had gathered or half gathered in the enthusiastic atmosphere generated between himself and his two legal advisers—in some respects at least he travelled like royalty—the night before, he could not help imagining that things might well turn out a very great deal worse than they had said was likely, or even possible. Like most people embroiled with the law he found it very difficult to concentrate sufficiently on what he was told about the technicalities and the dangers of his situation. Nor, although he had had several conversations about that matter too, did he know at what stage his friends the gentlemen of the press would feel constrained to take an interest in his agonies.

Fear and distaste inducing a desire to bring these conversations to an end and resulting in a pretence that he understood all that was being said to him were responsible for the fact that the Baron, normally so quick-witted and quite technically minded, understood so little of what he had been told about possible eventualities in either case.

A more or less complete ignorance of legal processes did not prevent him inventing scenarios for disaster of one kind or another, however; and since he had now given up worrying about the time, and had no other distractions to divert him, he soon suffused, mentally and physically, with shame for the outcomes and indignities the morning might hold.

WALRUS-MOUSTACHED COUNSEL FOR THE PROSECUTION. And during these months you gradually found yourself on terms of greater intimacy with him?
WITNESS. Yes, I did.
C FOR THE P. And your wife too, Mr O'Bogadain?
WITNESS. She became quite friendly with him, yes.
C FOR THE P. In fact it would be true to say that he gradually insinuated himself into your friendship?
WITNESS. It would.
C FOR THE P. And was the recipient of your hospitality on more than one occasion?
WITNESS. Yes.
C FOR THE P. And did he eventually tell you some story about his ancestry?
WITNESS. he did.
C FOR THE P. What was the purport of it?
WITNESS. The purport of it was that he was the grandson of

Richard Pigott, the forger.

C FOR THE P. Indeed. And did he say he had any proof of this?

ELDERLY JUSTICE. Hold on a jiffy, Mr Er. Is there any proof that he was a forger?

C FOR THE P. Well, we are naturally going to adduce proof, your honour. We are hopefully leading up to that.

JUSTICE. I am not talking about the accused. I am talking about Richard Pigott. Is there any proof that he was a forger? Was he ever tried for that offence in a court of law?

C FOR THE P. (after hurried consultation with solicitor) There seems to be some doubt about the matter, your honour.

JUSTICE. I think you'll find he wasn't. I have a certain knowledge of the period myself, and I think you'll find that he wasn't. Let's just call him a certain Richard Pigott, shall we?

C FOR THE P. I am grateful to your honour. I think I may say that everybody in this courtroom is familiar with your honour's explorations of interesting historical by-ways in a certain well-known publication. (To witness) And did he say he was the grandson of this Richard Pigott? Of a certain Richard Pigott?

WITNESS. He did.

C FOR THE P. Well, now. And did he say he had any proof of this?

WITNESS. He said he had some documents.

C FOR THE P. Documents. What sort of documents?

WITNESS. Er, letters. Receipted bills. Photographs.

JUSTICE. Photographs? That seems odd. What sort of photographs?

C FOR THE P. With your honour's permission we will come to them in a moment. (To witness) Did you believe him?

JUSTICE. Please be a little less ambiguous in your questioning, Mr Er. Do you mean did the witness believe the accused was the grandson of Richard Pigott or that the accused had documents?

C FOR THE P. The point is well taken your honour. (To witness) Did you believe he was Pigott's grandson?

WITNESS. I thought it quite possible.

C FOR THE P. Did you ask to see these documents?

WITNESS. I expressed interest in them. I believe I acquiesced in his suggestion that he should show them to me.

C FOR THE P. Why?

WITNESS. We were on terms of friendship. The matter was naturally of interest. Like his honour I too am a historian. I work in the Celtic Library.

C FOR THE P. Had the question of the purchase of the documents by the Library at this stage been mooted?

WITNESS. It had.

C FOR THE P. By whom was the possibility first suggested?

WITNESS. I believe by the accused.

ACCUSED. No no. That is untrue. I was not the first to suggest it.

JUSTICE. Silence please. (To accused, gently enough) Your turn will come. Don't worry about that.

C FOR THE P. (To witness) Your recollection is that he was the first to suggest the possible purchase of the documents by the Library?

WITNESS. It is.

C FOR THE P. And what did you say to that?

WITNESS. I said I thought the Library might be the right place for them. That is, if they were as described.

C FOR THE P. Had you any other motive besides the general interest of the documents to those who might use the Library and its fitness as a repository?

WITNESS. I wanted to do the accused a good turn if I could. I regarded him as my friend.

C FOR THE P. And do you still look upon him in this light?

WITNESS. I most certainly do not. I know a great deal more about him now than I did then. I know that he is an ingrate and a liar. I know that he wormed his way into my friendship for the purpose merely of getting money out of me in whatever way he could; that he used me as an instrument for deceiving and defrauding the Celtic Library; that he debauched my wife in the most insulting and off-hand fashion; that he is an altogether untrustworthy, unscrupulous, unreliable and insincere person whose relationship with almost everybody he has ever known has ended badly; that he talks a lot about art and does no work whatsoever; that he never liked me or my wife and cultivated the acquaintance only for what he could get, as he apparently does with everybody else he knows, including the present Minister for Justice Mr J. J. Fogarty and that innocent young girl, Susan Blackshaw, whom he has also attempted to make the instrument of his schemes ... .

ACCUSED. That's not fair. That's not true. I am among the least calculating of people. The average respectable member of society is much more calculating than I am. I blunder into everything like a blind man. In the early stages of my relationship with O'Bogadain and his wife I had no motives at all, good, bad or indifferent. It was, like everything else, drift ... And as for that girl you're talking about, Susan Blackshaw, when I met her first I had no idea at all she was connected with Pigott or anybody else ... .

It was, of course, true, he reminded himself, the courtroom vanishing from his mental screen, but what would the dear girl herself think? What was she to conclude when and if she read in the evening newspapers of today's proceedings, or heard about them from some eager informant? If O'Bogadain's testimony included reference to a tin box, perhaps a deed box or cash box, maybe even a dispatch box, but in any case embellished with the initials R.P., what would be Susan's reaction? Of course she too would think that he was a mere sordid conniver, a fraud and a chancer, the lowest of the low. Worse, she would think he was an eejit, a thooramalaun whose schemes inevitably degenerated into inconclusive and degrading farce. And she would probably be the sufferer for her connection with him. Beautiful, long-haired, long-legged, cool, competent Susan would become a mere figure of fun herself in the eyes of her friends and acquaintances.

And at this point, in order to avoid the hell of other chimeras, he chose that his imagination should dwell on the girl erotically rather than, so to speak, humanly. He conjured up a limb or two, even a convolution of limbs, and certain firm but yielding parts with their attendant apparel. He placed her, partly unclothed, in various circumstances, amorous or distressing.

Then he decided that this would not do. It was not fair, if only to the still existent possibility of more actual—say companionable—pleasures and conjunctions in the future. At the very least, and apart from moral considerations of a

16

perhaps rather Bloomsburyish kind, this was a poor time to be dissipating and weakening the possible erotic excitements that even thoughts of Susan could offer on other, more propitious private occasions.

Yet he knew from long experience that thoughts of women were really the only thing that would keep thoughts of disgrace and ridicule away; and he started therefore to cast around among those he had met or seen recently for another partner in misery. Perhaps because his imaginative faculty was at that moment weak he found, somewhat to his surprise, that the most plausible and easily created image was one of Osgur O'Bogadain's wife Fionnuala; and perhaps because his imaginative faculty was, at the moment, weak, he decided to accept it frizzy hair-do, myopic stare and all. It was almost a case of any port in a storm. In fact, though, when she was not present in person he found her, in spite of a certain flaccidity here and there apparent, just about attractive enough to do; and so, having accepted the image, albeit somewhat unwillingly, he began to toy with her. Undressing her as a mere prelude to conjunction, however, brought back memories of the almost totally unpleasurable occasions when he had in fact fucked her; and these being too painful, he decided to distance her and make her perform or something.

Accordingly he stood her alone in front of a crowd on some sort of raised stage or platform, clad in a brief two-piece costume, like a bathing suit, apparently waiting for a signal, either of commencement or release, and evidently highly conscious of her exposure to general regard.

So far, so good. But what, the Baron wondered, even as he warmed to her delicately boned, if, here and there, slightly flaccid body, was she required or expected to do? To dive? Or to strip off altogether? To contort herself, in dance or otherwise, or merely to stand and continue to suffer gaze? She would have to do something, for although at the moment she was betraying, in the way she licked her lips nervously with the tip of her tongue and smiled back at the crowd who watched her with a rather pathetic effrontery, satisfactory enough evidences of anxiety, discomposure, and perhaps even fear; action of some sort was quite evidently called for, not to say needed.

17

But whatever form it would have taken, Mrs O'Bogadain or at least her image, was at this point suddenly rescued or relieved from it by the Baron's growing awareness of a buzzing and drumming noise, quite unlike the swishing and swashing of heretofore which had the effect of recalling him to reality and nipping his incipient pleasure in what may be called the bud. It seemed to vary in pitch, if that was the term, and it faded and resumed mysteriously as well. With dismay he realised that this, now, was the commuters. But how long had they been at it? From the present volume of the noise they were already in full spate. How was it then that he had not heard them begin? Pre-occupied as he had been of course with that poor woman and her delicately boned, if, here and there, slightly flaccid body he might only just now have noticed the bloody noise. On the other hand it might only just now have started. It was the blasted birds all over again. There was now no evidence either way.

Uncertainty swept over him again. It could be any hour. He could be flung into durance vile this very morning for avoiding bail and have to remain there until the real trial came up. And then, most like, have to go back to the nick for the real term of imprisonment. In which case he would lose his sanity. He could face the sentence, whatever it might be, eventually. But he could not face this gaoling in the interval. It is the things that could have been easily avoided that unhinge the strongminded; and, in his way, the Baron was strong. Besides which he desperately needed the interval. One always needed an interval.

Then a known fact of contemporary civilisation came to his aid. The commuters did all wake at once, just like the birds. Just as the first cheep or whistle was succeeded at once by an unholy row, so the first gear change was followed at once by a general dash from the shelter of home to the shelter of work. It was possible, nay, it was likely, that he was listening to the beginnings of it.

But whether he had heard the bell ring and the tapes go up or not, the fact remained that the commuters had now started. The pig boy was in fact a lazy bastard who would wind up in the workhouse or in gaol; and the milkmen were as slack as

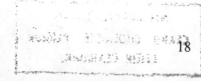

18

ever they had been in this part of the town. It was nine o'clock, on or about, give or take a quarter. He had better get up and face the music. Not to mention the mockery.

After standing uncertainly for a while in the dark little kitchen he decided to make tea. He knew his nervous system needed broader palliatives and his digestive more substantial nourishment, but it was at least a temporizing ritual and there was a tin of condensed milk somewhere. Whether tannic acid was the ticket or not an army does not march on an empty stomach.

The tea made, the cup washed, the tin pierced, the milk poured, he returned to the studio with the cup in his hand. He pulled back the curtains. It was broad day on a grey day and it was pouring rain. God knew what time it was. The hell with it. He would drink his tea. Normally the smell of turps and linseed oil, the scattering of rags, tubes and brushes in jam jars, the functional, unfurnished, untidy look of the place, would have soothed his spirit. But not now. They were reminders of Jonathen's industry (however misdirected) and his own impotence.

He walked over to the bed and sat down with his cup, turning his gaze resolutely away from the painting on the easel. He had not yet completed his toilet, but he would act on the assumption that it was about nine o'clock and have his tea in peace.

The Baron was a connoiseur of peace and of the intervals that provided it. He liked to spend, when work was out of the question, mornings in the snugs of remote public houses, to all others who knew him unknown, the brown mahogany around him, the price of two pints, a newspaper, the telephone unused and silent, sunlight peacefully fingering the woodwork, or just as good perhaps, the rain coming down in sheets, unassailed and unassailable, oblivious for an hour or two of the future and the past. He had a great capacity for peace. He liked the half hour in the privy with whatever reading matter was at hand, bits of strand confined by rocks which rendered you invisible from all sides but that of the sea, odd weeks in other

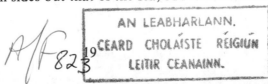

people's empty flats or cottages, time suspended on the top of a bus on the journey to an unpleasant destination, hospitalization of certain sorts.

Prison?

But even in these circumstances he needed something to occupy him, something to think on, something to read. There was a pile of books on the floor by the bed. He poked it gently with his foot. Jonathen had some peculiar reading matter. A small green volume, its binding ornamented with harps and shamrocks, attracted him. He picked it up. T. D. Sullivan. *Recollections of Troubled Times in Irish Politics.* Good God. What was a thing like this doing here? It was, you might say, very near the bone. Near the womb. It almost made you believe in some sort of supernatural agency, or, worse still, terrestrial. The Baron was much more afraid of terrestrial agencies than he was of supernatural. He might have been wrong in this, or, anyway, misguided, but he had never known the latter to do him any harm. The former were quite a different story.

Still, fearful as he was, he could not but open the volume now it and he were here. To his amazement and distress it fell open at a page which concerned the subject of nearly all his waking thoughts. These days.

"Pigott's next move was to turn on the man who had been giving him largesse time after time, and charge him with having contributed to his ruin, by showing him small kindnesses which he had imagined would lead up to larger and better things. Influenced by the hopes thus created, he said he had broken utterly with 'the other party', with the result that he now found himself completely stranded, without a ray of hope from any quarter. More than once he hinted at suicide as a way of ending his troubles. On June 26th, '83, after a long and fruitless series of applications for relief, he wrote:

'Dear Sir, —By this post I return you all the letters I ever received from you. My state of mind is such that I shall be tempted to do a desperate deed: and in that case these memorials of your good will and great kindness would be certain to fall into the hands of those who might misuse them. I am indeed in the lowest depths of despair: when a man sees his little children actually in want of food—at this season,

20

too—and is powerless to help them, he clearly but 'cumbereth the ground'.

To this epistle Mr Foster replied by return of post:
'I am sorry to hear of your difficulties, and enclose a five pound note, which may help to make your Christmas less dreary. At the same time I must add that I cannot afford to send you a further sum.' "

"His little children actually in want of food ... ." Tears welled up in the Baron's eyes. He saw the undoubtedly wet Christmas of 1883, rain streaming down the window-panes of some large, insufficiently furnished upstairs apartment which was known as the playroom. It had a bare board floor, a large table and two wooden chairs with arm rests. Here the boys usually had their tea, but today, the day after Christmas, there was no tea. They stood, two sturdy little men in knickerbockers, in front of the streaming window, the eldest's arm protectively round the youngest's shoulders. On the floor there were some broken toys and a tattered book, *"The Chatterbox Annual"*. There were no new toys. On the table stood two partially empty bowls of what he supposed to be gruel. In the fireplace the remains of a fire were still weakly smouldering.

But dammit, there was something wrong with this. What age would his father have been in 1883? Not for the first time he writhed in the throes of the uncertainties and improbabilities which are the inevitable result of adding material from a hitherto overlooked source to an already existing corpus of researched fact. It bloody well didn't work out. Or did it? According to his information his father had been born in 1880. Ah well, children could include a three year old. And his grandfather might have feared to seem mawkish by mentioning a babe, or babies.

Not for the first time, either, though, the Baron cursed De Valera, scourge of the Irish, who had ordered the burning of the Custom House and all the records of birth and ancestry that Ireland had to offer. Not that the Baron gave two hoots about the burning of the Custom House. In fact, in so far as he was called upon for an attitude, he rather approved of the burning of the Custom House and all records whatever. For the purpose of the particular piece of historical research on

21

which he himself had been engaged for so long, though, it could hardly be regarded as other than a nuisance. Ah well. He must in any case complete his toilet and get the hell out of here.

He got his tweed tie on and then the jacket of his suit. He rushed to the cupboard under the kitchen sink and dug out a small brush and a tin of polish. The polish was dried hard. He rested each shoe sole in turn on the edge of the sink and brushed blindly at the uppers, composing as he did so, of course, against his own wish, another scenario of the forthcoming court proceedings, complete with hitherto unimagined indignities, his invention once again unhampered by complete ignorance of legal matters.

His dread of these proceedings was at that moment far greater than his dread of the dooms that might, that would, eventually overtake him when the machinery of the law was set fully in motion. For proud spirits the dread of the immediate degradation is a great prophylactic against the dread of the ultimate disaster. What he feared at the moment was simple imminent indignity. Where worrying was concerned the Baron was of course a procrastinator; but he was also a proud man. Diurnal indignity, of which he suffered much, was to him a great shield against ultimate terrors.

In the large spotted pier glass (Susan? Would she?) in a corner of the studio he surveyed his raiment. The old W. J. Kelly tweed suit indestructible as always and the trousers not too bad now the jacket was on. Though he cared as little as possible for outward appearances the Baron's spiritual existence was dependent to some extent on these seven year old threads. The white shirt was passable and the thick orange tweed tie, acquired from the poet on the slopes of Mullaghcleevaun, contributed to the sober but not straitlaced artistic effect. Topped off by his bloody great curved nose, bushy eyebrows and tangled grey curly hair, the effect was almost of Protestant, private income art, courageous and condemnatory. "We have to dress the part," poor MacBryde used to say. "Otherwise they'll no believe in us."

He picked his money off the ledge of the easel where he had bestowed it the night before. It was eleven and ten pence ha'penny, the orange Irish ten bob note folded and sharp as a blade. At least he had openers he reflected, putting on his gaberdine, settling his cap on the side of his head and making (courageously) for the door.

22

Outside the eerie Irish greens of grass and shrub shone bright against the wet grey road and sky. It had almost stopped raining but his relief was tempered by the fact that there appeared to be an ominous thinness of inbound traffic over the hump of the bridge. The clock over Mooney's said twenty minutes to ten. He was late but he could be later. He took his place in the little wet queue for the bus.

At O'Connell Bridge it was five minutes to ten. He should run, he supposed; but he didn't run. He strode. Past the Dublin Bookshop and the Dairy Engineering Company, head up, in the rain, prepared to meet his fate.

He turned right by the Four Courts and went round the back where the District Courts are. The entrance was through a sort of bicycle shed, which struck him as fitting, the bicycle and the Irish policeman being properly associated together, as by the late na gCopaleen.

There were plenty of policemen in the narrow stoneflagged hall, mostly the young, athletic, glowing variety with pink faces and little wisps of blond hair on the cheekbones. Some of them were chatting in friendly fashion to their special delinquents, young and old, advising them and counselling them against bluff and trickery and futile attempts to face it out. Among them, like a portly liner surrounded by sinister destroyers and submarines, stood affable, urbane, summer-clad Mulvaney, and seeing his bulk the Baron felt considerably safer. But beside him stood the dark-haired, grey-eyed plain-clothes sergeant he already knew too well.

"Here he is now, Sergeant," said Mulvaney, smiling for the sergeant, raising a calm hand in greeting for himself. "No need for a warrant."

"Fine," said the sergeant. "We're all here so. I'll leave you to it then," he added, looking the Baron straight in the eye, as policemen, oddly enough, do. Where do they get that honest, concerned, probing look? he wondered. It is not from straight dealing anyway, he thought with some bitterness, though he felt guilty for the thinking so. The sergeant was a physically attractive, dominating, dependable seeming fellow, like a school prefect, and a little wish stirred in the Baron to be on the same side as he was, even indeed to be associated in some enterprise of danger and comradeship with him. But he felt guilty for that too.

Mulvaney turned to him, smiling in benediction. "How do you feel?" he asked, smiling.

The Baron became, against his wish, a little curt. "Oh, all right," he said. "How about yourself?"

"Pretty ropey, pretty ropey," Mulvaney said serenely. "We had a lot to drink."

"We had that," said the Baron, mollified, and then anxiously, too anxiously for his own taste, he added: "Listen, are you sure this is going to be all right? I mean are you certain that nothing can happen today?"

Mulvaney laid a placid, reassuring hand on his shoulder. "I think I can promise you," he said, "what Merlin promised Arthur."

The Baron waited. It would come. Mulvaney smiled soberly on him. The Baron could wait no longer. "What was that?" he asked.

"That you will come safe, speak with the mighty, and go safe."

"H'mm," said the Baron.

Smiling with enjoyment, the other then took him by the arm and controlled him gently towards the side of the passageway. "I'm just waiting for Toby," he said. "I want a final word with him. Nothing much," he added reassuringly. "Just a matter of tactics." He looked without impatience towards the door. "The fellow's late," he said serenely.

"I was nearly much later myself," began the Baron, "having neither clock nor watch ... ."

"Here he is now," said Mulvaney, raising a contented hand in greeting.

MacNeice appeared in the, briskly hesitated a second and then came forward, full-fed lips pursed, pampered fingers clasped round some papers over his chest, the wings of an invisible gown floating momentarily behind him.

"Ah," said Mulvaney. "Counsel is here."

MacNeice smiled at the edges of pursed lips. Then he

24

assumed a portentous air. The Baron observed Mulvaney assuming gravity also. The bastards, he thought. We are going to have some role-playing. And my only role is that of the poor bollocks in trouble.

"Let's go in here for a moment," said MacNeice.

He led them into a sideroom with a bare floor, a bench running round the walls and an empty fireplace. The two grimy windows were barred. The room was distempered green, like the hall.

In the far corner a sallow youth with long, pale, watered hair brushed into a duck's tail stood with bowed and abject head while a lawyer with a brief-case spoke to him slowly, sternly, emphatically. The youth emanated ignorance and fear. As, thought the Baron, I am beginning to do myself.

But MacNeice began to speak.

"You haven't heard?" he said, looking from one to the other.

Both shook their heads.

"Friend O'Bogadain," said MacNeice, "has had a breakdown. A bad case, apparently. He was removed to Saint John of God's since we saw him last, and by all accounts he's in a straight jacket."

The Baron's relief was for one reason or another enormous, but, even as relief swept over him, he thought: may God forgive me.

MacNeice raised a hand as if someone had been about to interrupt. "And," he said slowly, "they can't find the documents."

"Phew," said Mulvaney. "That alters the picture."

"They have hunted," said MacNeice, "high and low. Upstairs and down, and damn the document can they find."

"Well now," said Mulvaney. "Well now. What are they asking us to do?"

"Surely," asked the Baron, "that's the end of it? I mean if the bloody man's gone mad and they haven't got the stuff, it's all over."

MacNeice shook a well-groomed head.

"Alas no," he said. "There are too many state agencies involved. And they're out of pocket. It's by no means over.

25

However, they are asking for a month. In the circumstances of course, they're entitled to ask and in a manner of speaking they're entitled to get it. But here's my idea."

He glanced around and, lowering his voice, went on. "They have been thrown very much into disarray of course, but in a month's time they may well be ready again. The patient may even be recovered. At least they'll be briefed, and they may have the goods. But supposing ... ." He looked the Baron accusingly in the eye. "Supposing I lure them into a formal adjournment till Monday morning merely, and supposing on Monday we could produce the goods, the genuine article, the real and only alley daley? At the very least we could say there was a mistake made; offer them our genuine lode, probably worth much more than the miserable sum that has changed hands for the fake one, and enquire what they had to beef about. In the absence of the unbalanced O'Bogadain, and being in such disarray, I am as certain as a man could be that they would leap at it. The polis would. The lawyers would. And the apparent instigator of these proceedings, the raving lunatic, is if I may say so, in no position to object."

"But ... ." began the Baron.

"But me no buts, my dear Baron," interposed MacNeice sternly, raising a plump white hand. "The box and its contents must now be produced. The box, the box and nothing but the box," he continued smiling, "has to be dragged forth from its hiding place and offered to the state as the Baron Ponsonby .gift and bequest to take the place of all other alleged boxes and their contents whatever. Then by God Roddy," he added warmly, "you are a free man, and a free man with a proven and proud ancestry at that."

The Baron looked from one to the other in mute appeal. "But," he said, "I haven't got the box. They won't give it to me."

MacNeice leaned forward so that the Baron received a whiff of something or other—cachou nuts perhaps?—from his full-fed lips. "Burgle for it, if necessary," he said. "Break and enter."

"He's right, you know," said Mulvaney, laying a gentle

hand on the Baron's shoulder. "Now's the time to strike home, while they're running unsighted. To-morrow. This week-end. To-day. Any later may be too late."

MacNeice jabbed the Baron in the chest with a plump index finger. "Burgle for it," he said coldly. "You know where it is."

Mulvaney looked towards the door. "They're going in," he said. "The good Justice is usually exactly twenty minutes late. You'll intimate to them then that we've been taken by surprise ourselves, Toby, and suggest Monday as a *quid pro quo*?" MacNeice nodded, moving towards the door. "Leave it to me," he said.

"And what do I have to do?" asked the Baron desperately.

"Just get the box," said MacNeice over his shoulder.

"But this morning I mean," said the Baron. But they were already ahead of him, moving towards the door, in cheerful converse about something else.

"You'll hear your name called," said MacNeice turning.

In the courtroom across the corridor the Justice was already on the bench and was saying something which sounded rather cross. He looked like an indigent, rather dissipated, family doctor of the old school.

The Baron stood uncertainly inside the door, among a gaggle of tall policemen, then moved down the side aisle towards the back and leaned against the wall, an already broken man.

Whatever the Justice was saying and however cross it was, it caused a general, modified laugh. The youth with the duck's tail sat inside the door of the dock near the Baron. He too was laughing, his head bowed, glancing sideways for support or encouragement, as, the Baron remembered, the objects of the schoolmaster's sarcasms used to do. The Baron looked away. There is a point beyond which some victims are more offensive than their persecutors.

The walls of the courtroom, like those of the place they had just left, were distempered a pale sickly green. The windows were high, dusty, barred. At the back, behind a railing, were some raised benches, occupied by a lot of shabbily dressed people, young and old. From their would-be alert expressions they appeared to be participants or sympathizers rather than members of the general public. At the moment they registered a sort of wretched anxiety to be amused. Smiling and nudging each other they indicated their understanding and appreciation of the Judge's testy joke, whatever it was.

He watched the pale youth leave the dock. The Baron gathered that he had just been sent to gaol for six months but he was grinning and winking at someone in the spectators' benches. Looking elsewhere as he was, the youth did not go very promptly down the steps and an elderly fat policeman took him by the arm and pushed him. The youth grinned and wagged more sheepishly than before and the fat old policeman frowned and muttered angrily, looking towards the Judge on the bench as he did so and managing to be both bully and sycophant at once. Christ, thought the Baron, gazing around at the sickly green walls and the sickly anxious people, they manage to create sordidity all right. My little efforts are only in the ha'penny place.

Then he became aware that everybody round about was looking at him. MacNeice was standing up in the lawyers' benches and making a stern face at him across the court. His detective sergeant, who was among the police near the door, had turned round towards him and was gesturing insistently towards the dock. His own name, enunciated some time before, penetrated his consciousness. His arm was grasped by the elderly policeman and he was pushed roughly up the step. His time had come.

They were all looking at him now, idly or curiously, and there was some conversation going on between the Judge and others, but he could not hear what was being said.

"Sit down," said the policeman beside him. The Baron did so.

A man who sat at a table in front of the Judge's dais, presumably a clerk of some kind, stood up and showed his testiness something in a large book like a ledger, running his finger down the page, tapping it, apparently urging something. The Judge frowned. A young man who had been standing up at a table near MacNeice sat down. The clerk swivelled the book part way round as if to verify something for himself and then turned it back to the Judge who transferred his frown round the court and let it rest eventually on the Baron.

"Stand up," whispered the policeman furiously. The Baron did so, clutching his coat and his cap. The Judge moved the frown away and settled it finally on MacNeice.

"Sit down," whispered the policeman, with contempt. The Baron sat down as MacNeice stood up.

"You have no objection to that Mr ehhh?" asked the Judge.

MacNeice leaned forward slowly, propping himself against the table on an extended middle finger.

"Well my client is naturally anxious—most anxious—to have the matter disposed of."

"Doubtless he is."

"This is naturally a time of great circumstantial unsettlement for him."

"Mental too, I daresay," said the Judge. "We're all doing our best to accommodate him I'm sure, but there appear to be certain difficulties about proceeding due to the illness of a vital witness and some consequential difficulty about exhibits. I am told we will know more about the possibilities on Monday morning and I am sure we all echo that hope."

"All ... right," said MacNeice, suddenly and naturally sitting down and producing a pen.

The clerk leaned over the book again and the Judge wrote something. Then he looked up under his eyebrows. "Continuing bail?" he asked and without apparently waiting for anybody's assent wrote something else. The elderly policeman plucked at the Baron's sleeve. He stumbled gladly from the dock. At the door he was joined by Mulvaney. "You'll just have to step into the office and sign the bail form," he said, smiling. "Then you're as free as the air of morning."

He guided the Baron through another door, into a room where a policeman stood typing at a counter. As he signed the form eventually presented to him the Baron saw by the watch on the policeman's hairy wrist that it was five minutes to eleven. In five minutes he could be in the blessed peace and security of the pub, safe for a while at least from the barbarisms of circumstance and the law.

Furthermore, when he came out of the building with Mulvaney and MacNeice the sun was shining metallically in a sky which contained large areas of blue and tumbled grey clouds with pale edges were breaking all round to reveal more. Light flashed from the wet road and parked motor cars. Broad summer was all about them. But the Baron's problems were by no means over.

"Anybody care for a drink?" he asked, fingering the sharp edges of the note and the milled edges of the silver in his pocket.

"I have a running-down action," said MacNeice.

"And I," said Mulvaney, "have another client beyond."

His briefly raised spirits were lowered again. Apart from anything else he could not face the chances of such a day as this with the money he had. He would have to ask Mulvaney for a pound. And he wanted to talk about the morning's developments. While he hesitated, however, the latter said kindly:

"Unless you'd care to wait for me? We should get on in half an hour or so and the whole thing will only take a few minutes."

"I'll wait all right if you're sure you'll be along," said the Baron.

"If you wait over there," said Mulvaney, pointing to a lowfronted, common enough pub on the corner, "I'll be along in half an hour or less."

"O.K." said the Baron. "I haven't read the paper yet, anyway."

He turned to MacNeice, who was adjusting a gold tie clasp with indulgent fingers. "Thank you again, Toby, by the way," he said. "That was good news this morning, wasn't it?" he asked, and then, conscious that he had used the wrong phrase added weakly: "From our point of view I mean."

"It was only good news if we take advantage of the circumstances," said MacNeice grimly. "As of this moment we have the initiative. Your friend is off his chump and presumably under sedation or even possibly restraint. That means they're on the hop and will be until Monday. A month or two later—and they could easily have it put back for that length of time—you'll be in the same danger as you stand in

30

today, which is no light or laughing matter. From what has already been explained to you, you will have grasped that it is the box on which, if I may hazard a metaphor, the whole thing hinges. You say there may be extra-legal methods of procuring it. Use them. Now. To-day. Or, at latest, to-morrow."

He smiled warmly, extending a well-manicured hand. "Glad to be of service, old fellow." he said. "I'll be at home over the week-end. I expect to hear from you. Don't let the side down."

And as he went, Mulvaney said: "He's right, you know. We have a chance of turning the whole thing inside out now. See you in half an hour."

Beside the pub was a newspaper shop where the Baron procured a couple of journals, one English, one Irish, to solace his wait. Then he entered the licensed premises, the newspapers tucked under his arm. The interior, low, cool and dim, with a feeling of having just been sprinkled and swept about it, as befitted the time of day and its proximity to opening time, met his wants and suited his mood. They even had Roses lime juice to put in his gin; and now, for the first time, seated in this cool interior, he was able to reflect on the news he had heard. O'Bogadain had gone out of his mind. He had done a Lady Macbeth. No, that wasn't right. He, himself, was the guilty party. Only he could or should do a Lady Macbeth, calling on the perfumes of Arabia to sweeten his little hand. But the fact was that he had not suffered any remorse whatever for some considerable time now; and, far from causing him any, this new turn of the wheel caused him considerable satisfaction.

But this was a change, for after the deed had been first done he had suffered a good deal of remorse; and thoughts of Osgur O'Bogadain and his wife Fionnuala had afflicted him through many a sleepless hour. It would even seem that once the mechanism of the law was set in motion against anybody their guilt-sufferings diminished, being replaced by mere thoughts-of-punishment-sufferings, in a way much easier to bear. And he was pretty sure that if he was actually sent to prison his guilt-feelings would disappear entirely in favour of mere circumstance-sufferings. He had, in a sense, that much to look forward to. This characteristic of human psychology showed that there was something wrong with the whole punishment system. Including, you might say, the after life. It was obviously preposterous to suggest that you would or could go on loving God while he continued to torture you atrociously on the head of some ever more remote offence; and to suggest that you would go on feeling guilty about him and whatever you might have done to his delicate sensibilities while every moment that passed proved his power, vindictiveness and wellbeing and your absolute helplessness in his hands, was even more preposterous. It was not in human nature.

The thought restored his good humour. Content that something had been established, he turned to the newspapers he had bought.

In O'Turk's too it was, naturally, just after opening time. The narrow, high-ceilinged bar of the establishment was deserted except for a solitary customer with a pint and a barman who was running a cloth up and down the pump handles. Then the glass door at the end was pushed in and a long face culminating in a large nose, horn-rimmed spectacles and tweed cap peered suspiciously round it. For a few moments no other portion of the surveyor's anatomy was visible. Then the door opened further and he came in, reached a stool in two strides of his enormous feet, mounted it and made twitching motions of his huge shoulders as he glared at the barman.

"Has the Baron been in?"

"Haven't seen him so far." The barman leaned forward, executing wide circular swathes with a cloth on the counter. "Come to think of it now I haven't seen him for a few days. He must be lyin' low. What'll I give you?"

"The best of his play, the bollocks. Give us a glass of port."

"A glass of port. Any particular variety?"

"Oh just port. Port. Any port in a storm."

The original customer, pint raised in his red fist, laughed politely.

"A glass of port," said the barman again. He placed a goblet on the counter, selected a bottle from the shelf and poured some of the translucent, maroon liquid it contained; paused, considered for a moment, head aslant, and poured again. "There you are doctor," he said. "Vintage."

"I hear he's in England," said the first customer.

"And I hear he's in trouble," said the one addressed as doctor sternly, folding his arms with an air of certitude.

"Trouble? What sort of trouble? What's he been up to now?" asked the barman over his shoulder as he replaced the bottle on the shelf.

"Something I heard. Somethin' I heard on me travels." The speaker spun a half a crown on the cork-topped counter, flattened the spinning object suddenly with a wide, heavy hand and added: "You'll be hearing about it."

The barman half turned, picked up the coin in a swung right hand, operated the cash register, dropped the coin into the out-thrust drawer, extracted some lesser pieces and placed them on the counter without turning round.

"That'll be the day," he said cryptically.

"You'll be hearing about it all right I misdoubt me not," said the port drinker. "Ay, and maybe even reading about it in the public prints."

"Do you tell me?" asked the barman. He threw his cloth on to a biscuit tin, turned, lifted a half-filled pint off the ring and drew slowly on the pump handle, partially suspending his weight from it. "It wouldn't by any chance be rubber or anything like that?" he asked, looking sideways at the port drinker.

"It could be something of that ilk. Something of that genus."

"H'mm." The barman finished off the pint with a last, slow, gentle pressure on the handle and placed it in front of the other customer. "There's the second one requested," he said.

Then he placed his hands on the edge of the counter wide apart and looked the original speaker in the eye.

"Mind you," he said, "it wouldn't surprise me very greatly what sort of messing he'd get up to in some respects, for he is a bit of a messer. But on the other hand he's an honest sort of a fellow too, and to tell you the truth it would surprise me if he deliberately done anybody."

"Or if he got the chance," put in the pint drinker.

The barman laughed. The third party did not.

"Is it trouble with the law he's in?" asked the barman.

"Is there any other kind of trouble?" queried the one addressed. "Sticks and stones may break my bones but only writs can hurt me. The law is what matters. The rest is only prestige stuff." He spread a newspaper out on the counter and battered it into subservience with a large hand. "Never you mind what sort it is and don't ask me any more about it anyhow, but that's the fact of the matter and I'm only telling you what I heard. Naw bock lesh."

The other two were silent, gazing at him with respect.

Then the barman took his own newspaper from the shelf behind him and held it, open wide, at arm's length.

"The yokes on the buses," he said. "The swords of light. They were imported from Holland."

In St Stephen's Green it was broad summer, the sudden expanse of sky calmly patrolled by diaphanous clouds, greyish, but bright-white-bordered. The Baron, parted from Mulvaney and the richer by a pound, walked in warm sunlight towards the top of Dawson Street.

Though the sun was pleasant on his back, there were plenty of girls about, and the scene and the hour would normally have delighted him, he walked almost oblivious of his surroundings. There had been something unsatisfactory about the morning's procedures: more unsatisfactory even than unpleasant. What did they think they were up to? If something had to be done to malefactors who caused misery to people like Osgur—not to mention his wife Fionnuala—and diddled the state out of money—their courts and gaols were not the answer. Those institutions merely increased the collective sordidity. And the object, from all parties' points of view, should surely be to decrease it, sordidity being the common enemy. That some sort of punishment or restraint might be necessary, however, he was prepared to admit; and though his was not the responsibility, he sought now in the sunlight to devise alternative methods. Public exhibitions and punishments of various kinds, the stocks, dunce caps and placards, these would harness the powerful forces of remorse and shame. According to Doctor Joyce Brothers, whom he had (also) been reading in Jonathen's, being made to stand naked while others were clothed was a very ancient and primal sort of punishment. Whippings of half-naked women at the cart's tail of course gave satisfaction to many citizenry who had no interest whatever in justice or atonement. H'mm.

He brought his mind back to the problem. He thought of labour groups, housed in cosy hutments in the barren and beautiful places of the west, reclaiming mountain-side by day under the eternally changing sky, reading Tolstoy under the roof at night by hissing oil lamps; the conscription of delinquents for nasty or dangerous jobs such as schoolteaching or lavatory attending; negotiations with America and the United Arab Republic, or, better still, Israel and North Vietnam, for the induction into various foreign legions of those of a military cast of mind, provided their willingness was assured; most of all, though, he thought of himself and his colleagues in the dictatorship hearing hard cases, pardoning, encouraging, reassuring. He came to the microphone and announced the imminent dissolution of the prison system in favour of other methods of atonement, or punishment, or protection of the innocent, or whatever the point was supposed to be, these methods to be devised by committees of decent fellows and detailed later. He announced further that the state was unwilling any longer to assume the burden of the concept of Justice. But then he thought, and the thought chilled the sunlight, of the fact that he really might go to gaol after all was said and done.

"If that box is still in fact in existence, and if there is any way of getting hold of it before Monday morning," Mulvaney had said, "for Heaven's sake, do. If this girl of yours can help, so much the better, but one way or another it really is essential to get hold of it and to get hold of it now when we're only dealing with officialdom and the law and not with people motivated by other feelings. Besides, think of the effect on your own psychology of having the whole matter put on a publicly acknowledged, legal basis. It has created a bit of a hiatus, you know. You are a bit in suspension. And that is not to speak of the gaol sentence which really and truly is a possibility. I mean three or four years out of your life would be no bloody joke, would it? I don't want to frighten you, but that could easily be the outcome. So why not have a bash at it? To-day?"

And, accordingly, the Baron had promised action this day. Why a matter which threatened only himself had to be put on a promissory basis to someone else before he would do the needful was just one of those things about his psychology which he understood without understanding the reasons. But so it was. Other parties, standing somehow in *loco parentis,* had to be brought in, and a bit of guilt had to be created before he would act; but anyway, promise he had; and act he would, this blessed summer day.

For that reason now he mooched along Merrion Street past O'Neill's, where Osgur had once been wont to sit amongst his cronies. It would be nice if he could turn this present absence of guilt into positive hatred of the party who, whatever wrongs had been done him, had, after all, called in the law. Or had he? The Baron made a conscious effort to hate him, bourgeois bilingual bollocks that he was. But he lacked the gift, common enough among people he knew, of hating those whom he had injured. Osgur was nevertheless typical of the really objectionable element in this bloody country, the liberalised Gaeligoireach apparatchik who, far more than profiteers or politicians, had it sucked dry; and against whom all weapons and deceits were justified, even if only as instants of the people's vengeance to come. He thought of the long, serious, national-culturist face, the thin walled suburban house with the department store reproductions and the single, bad, original picture. He called to mind the allegedly Dublin jokes and the inner circles of the Vatican jokes, the stilted, would-be ironical English (derived from Myles's worst efforts) deployed in O'Neill's on a Saturday night, where he sat, a prince among peers because of the job and the monograph, happy in the knowledge that he had a place in the scheme of things, that he was the scheme of things. The job in the Celtic Library gave him, of course, immense public status to begin with, far more than that possessed by the poor mere writers of the Baron's acquaintance, and the single publication crowned him with laurel. The Baron thought of the endless deployment of alleged learning, historical and otherwise; he thought of the literary pontificatings shamelessly indulged in even in the presence of the arch-poet; he called to mind the accent used for displays of learning and the broader accent used for native anecdote; he remembered, alas, Fionnuala, whom he first had taken, clothed and moaning, across the bed, her housewife's head hanging over the edge, while Osgur talked on downstairs. And at this point, he realised, it was not Osgur he hated but himself.

He turned into Merrion Street in the still noonday sunlight and passed government buildings. To change the subject he tried to think of the Ministers of the far away Free State, barricaded in there behind barbed wire and bulks of wood and sandbags. Cosy enough, he thought, to be lying on the camp bed discussing matters with men of equal distinction over a drop of D.W.D. while the odd shot echoed through the leafy summer twilight. Were they barricaded in there before or after the others got Mick? Lonely drop of D.W.D. without him. Life and soul. He not only had a presence but an absence too. The God forsaken country had felt it ever since. Before and after. Photograph of the gun carriage passing here, horses' hooves polished for the occasion. Clip, clop.

In the British time all of Ireland was governed from here and the Custom House and the Castle, Mr Birrell commuting on the mailboat, tables for the Chief Secretary, his man and his detective in the saloon. Usual bottle of Beaujolais and ballon of bisquet. Bursts of wet over the bows in the bay. Bad night I'm afraid Mr Birrell, sir. Cloak and shooting cap at Holyhead, then clickety click, dundeddy ump, as snug as a bug in a rug all the way to Euston. Now they needed to demolish half the town to accommodate the apparently necessary, native, Gaeligoireach apparatchik.

Inevitably, he thought again of Osgur; and desperately he tried again to hate, but it would not work. It was indeed himself he hated: his visits to the house, her unending, intrusive chatter, himself beside Osgur in O'Neill's being affable to his friends and accepting drinks from all quarters, the night they had sat together in the corner there while he told Osgur all about the box and the documents in the box, the trembling drunken day when he had at long last produced some of them for inspection and the subsequent one when he had waited in the outer office for Osgur to smilingly produce the countersigned government cheque. Oh God. He stopped, faced the ground and deliberately attempted to drive guilt from him.

But had he not lied to the poor man, played the ingrate with him, cheated him—or at least his masters—made what is sometimes called love to his wife in a largely pleasureless and therefore immoral way and now, at last, driven him into the looney bin?

He lifted his head.

One diaphanous cloud drifted across the sky at the end of the street.

The arrangement of roofs at the corner pleased him. Opposing, intersecting planes, just below his level. He stayed where he was for a moment, pleased, frustrated, distressed. Some day, when he had finished with his planks, he would become the master of roof planes. Soulages how are you. It showed you how little they knew. On, dammit, on. Before he could even think about painting again he had to get free of this present awful brulement.

He went on again northward, downhill, towards the end of the street, number one Merrion Square and the bus route to Dun Laoghaire.

A number 7a. That would do. But could he go through with this? Did he not need and deserve at least another drink? The Lincoln's Inn? No, he was going out there to-day to lay hands on his inheritance, the black box that was his birth-right. If he didn't go now he would never go. Besides, Susan had marked his card. The coast, as he knew, was clear. The bus squealed and sighed to a stop beside him. Admiral without epaulettes, he went on board.

At Booterstown the Baron crossed over to the other side of the bus. He did not wish to see Knockley College, its buildings and its groves and playing fields, for him a specially laid out garden of remembrance. There was the time he had been discovered to have nits in his hair. The time he had been walking round the infirmary with shit on his pyjama pants without knowing it. The time he had left the letter from his aunt in the lavatory. And then there were his various enthusiasms: the time of his letter in "Our Boys"; the time he had made the speech to the debating society about love as the guiding principle in the universe without realising that he was being laughed at; the time he had led the strike: all the various impulsive gestures which had turned out in the end to be precipitants of absurdity and shame. Shamefulness and absurdity had become the ruling principles early. He had lived five years under their governance here.

Even though he had decided not to, the Baron now sneaked a look as the bus swung past the castle, the driveway, the football pitch and the tower with the statue of the blessed virgin, she who presided over five hundred boys' misery and shame and loved them for it. It seemed in any case fitting that he should salute the place to-day, for it was on the occasion of the strike he had led at Knockley College that the secret of his ancestry had first in part been confirmed to him; and of course it was his knowledge of his accursed ancestry that had led directly to his present troubles.

The strike had taken place one winter evening when the rest of the world was going home in lighted trams to rashers and radio programmes by a glowing fire. Aroused to protest by himself and others the seniors had lined up in the cold dusk, by the wall at the top of the gravelled recreation yard, and refused to go into study.

An injustice had been committed. That was the phrase they used. He had probably originated it. A fellow had been punished for whistling at one of the skivvies. But he hadn't whistled. Or he had whistled but not at her. The Baron couldn't remember. But he could remember her. She was a tall, darkhaired, strong-haunched colleen with a mischievous eye, about the only personable thing of the female persuasion there was around, the rest being malformed half-wits, charity slaves, as she was too, but somehow not malformed. Quite the contrary in fact. Very beautifully formed indeed. And accordingly the Baron had often and often summoned her to his bed at night. In imagination of course. He did not, however, imagine what are called intimacies with her. The visual played a large part in his pleasure and it was his nocturnal wont to put her in situations where he could stand off a bit and have a look. This involved bathing suits and degrees of undress and brief costumes such as he had sometimes seen worn in theatrical performances of one kind or another. But these situations were often also ones of discomfort or even risk for her, and she was almost invariably required or expected to do things which were either physically or mentally dangerous or repugnant to her: to dive for pearls in a shark-infested sea, to wrestle with other females in a fairground booth, to be partner to an incompetent knife-thrower, to cross Niagara Falls on a tightrope or merely to parade or dance in front of a male audience, himself of course in the front row. That's the trouble, he thought now, with enforced celibacy. We become depraved voluptuaries of the imagination, craving ever acuter stimuli, before we can even walk. But I am talking like a liberal fraud, he said to himself, blaming everything on the system. Seriously though, what in fact was to blame, supposing the word blame applied, for the nature of his infantile imaginings? Had the contents of the box anything to do with it? No, for of course many of them preceded the box and were present, so far as he could remember, in infancy itself, or at least while he was still in short trousers. The truth was that nobody knew, whatever they might say. Hereditary predisposition perhaps?

Anyway, he who had often made her some sort of a victim in his lewd imaginings protested the injustice of anybody else being thought to have lusted after her, when of course he had not done so. At clandestine meetings among the green sheds of the seniors' lavatory he had been a leader, a manipulator of men, one with a policy and a faction. He could still remember the ecstasy of it. It made you feel luminous or something.

The injustice was first discussed after morning classes and an articulate and forthright Baron had found himself readily listened to. As the day wore on, opinion about what should be done became more radical, but the Baron, slightly intoxicated now with power, was always well abreast of it, and was a principal member if not the leader of the faction which favoured the strike weapon rather than the more moderate round-robin of mere protest. Gesticulating, sincere, eloquent, humorous and dashing, he was the typical lightweight of revolution, the Camille Desmoulins of the green sheds. And in the end the centres of power had wavered before the ebullient surge of feeling. In the cold dusk of the recreation yard there had been a promise by the Dean of a further investigation—a matter perhaps complicated, though nobody seemed to notice that, by the dismissal of the skivvy, doubtless to walk the streets of Birmingham and become, in palpable fleshly being this time, the patient sufferer of lusts or vehicle for the implementation of lewd imaginings more unpleasant even than the Baron's. Anyway, that evening there had been a sort of yielding or apology or promise of redress on the part of the authorities; and they had all gone back to the study hall.

But the following morning, after breakfast in the refectory, had come the counter-revolution, the white terror. Father Freshman, the President himself, had made an entrance and a speech.

At the top of this long green distempered room there had been a raised dais with a crucifix hanging on the wall above it. Here, under the representation of the divine cadaver the priests immediately in charge normally ate; and here now Father Freshman stood, his cape thrown back, his hands for the moment thrust into his girdle, his bald red skull throbbing with rage.

There was a slight scuffling of chairs, some coughing, a dying run of talk. Then Father Freshman leaned diagonally backwards across the table and banged the bell thereon with the palm of his right hand. An absolute silence fell, even those caught in uncomfortable positions afraid to move. Erect again, the holy father frowned terribly, the red skin of his skull furrowing vertically down to black eyebrows. He waited, as Lord Melbourne advised Queen Victoria to do on such occasions, and he succeeded in filling the wait with such intensity that any power to resist what he might say was already paralyzed. Like Queen Victoria, he had of course the whip hand.

"What form of address to adopt," he said then, "I do not

know. Up to last night I could have addressed you as my dear boys, or my dear younger brothers in Christ, my dear charges. Up to last night it seemed that we were all here Christian members of one community living under the roof of this house together in Christian amity and belief. Boys might be bold and even sinful. Boys might do things which deserved punishment and it would then become the duty of the Deans under my Presidency to punish them, with the cane or the strap or the whip if necessary. This painful duty accomplished however we could still be reasonably confident that the boy. had not wavered from fundamental obedience to the Christian principles which the fathers and I have tried to implant in every heart.

"But what can I say now? What can I say now?" he shouted rising on his toes.

He paused and continued more quietly. "Every boy in this community came from a good Catholic home. As you all know before you were accepted here these homes were visited by the fathers of the order, visited to see that homes and parents were what we might naturally expect them to be, god-fearing, right-thinking and representative of Irish Catholicism at its best."

Touting for custom, the same fathers were when they visited, as the Baron even then well knew, but could not at that moment bring himself to think, thus experiencing for the first time how fear will paralyze even the powers of secret mental affirmation, a melancholy matter demonstrated again and again in our time.

"Were we wrong?" screamed Father Freshman. "Were we wrong about any of these homes? Were we wrong about any of the parents who in some cases have made financial sacrifices, in some cases have had to forego other ... possibilities"—he had appeared almost to be about to say pleasures—"in some cases have had to scrimp on this and save on that in order to send boys here? Is it possible that the fathers were wrong and that some of the homes they went into were not good, holy, god-fearing Catholic homes at all? Or"—he swept his right hand outwards, palm down, fingers extended to take in everyone there—"or is it possible that boys who came from such homes, homes where the fear of God is truly in the parents' hearts and the name of God and his holy mother on the parents' lips—can behave like ingrates, like deceivers, like wretches beyond comparison, almost, terrible though it be to say it, like Spanish atheists, Spanish communists, wretched Spanish enemies of our holy mother the Church and the priests who serve her every day of their lives?"

The silence that followed this was another awful presence in the refectory and Father Freshman paused to allow it to aid him, hands back in the girdle, eyes flashing under red skull and coal black brows, shoulders squared under thrown back cape, the whole terror-inspiring figure four square against the by comparison somewhat flaccid and colourless body of the revolutionary on the cross.

Since the smell of burning churches had already been wafted by the newspapers from Spain to Ireland, it was a terrible charge and all here knew it. Father Freshman allowed himself to pace a trifle right and left, head slightly bowed. Then he faced them again.

"Can this be the case?" he demanded. "That there are ingrates and deceivers and atheistic communists amongst you? Can it? Do I have to entertain the thought that boys from homes like yours should be guilty of the kind of attitude towards god-given authority that we read about in the unfortunate newspapers which have to report events in Spain, that I heard about when I returned to this house last night? I was tired. I had been travelling all day. I had attended the consecration of a bishop on behalf of the order but I returned ready for prayer and sleep with the feeling of coming home that all who live in this great house should have. And what did I discover? What did I find? That in my absence, while my back was turned, the discipline of the house had been scorned and jeered at, the good order of the house had been overturned and overthrown, the good name of the house that generations of priests and boys together built up had been threatened, jeopardised and imperilled."

White-faced all stared at him. White-faced, the Baron stared, a vein in his neck pulsing while the priest's bald pate in righteous anger pulsed. But for the Baron there was worse to

43

come; as, even at that age, he might have known, there always was.

"It is probable that the majority of the boys who took part in this outrage were misled. I prefer to believe that they proved themselves nothing more wicked than supine weaklings and sinful cowards. Realising as they must have done in their heart of hearts that they were doing wrong, they allowed themselves to be led and bamboozled and tricked by a few miscreants and scoundrels, a few slackers and loafers whose horrible false vanity would not allow them to admit that they could not compete with others in certain manly ways, certain studious ways, certain considerate and fair and just and ordinary ways and who therefore sought by high talk and scoffing and sneering and jeering at authority to bring down the good order and decent rule of this house and make themselves important by whatever disruption of studious conduct and manly practices and obedient behaviour and athletic pastimes they could bring about."

It was, the Baron thought now, a pretty fair definition of a certain type of revolutionary, himself perhaps included. But Father Freshman was not done, nor done with him in particular.

"Let me tell you the history of one of these boys, one of these miserable boys," he continued, in a tone of such scorn that it almost included compassion. "He does not know this history. But the time has come perhaps to enlighten him, although I will not mention his name now, he will be told in private who and what he is. He will be told because the telling may teach him something about the great Christian consideration and kindness of the bishops and priests of this country and the fathers of this order, a Christian consideration and a Christian charity without which he would not be here." He raised both his hands to heaven suddenly and shouted: "Without which he would not be here to play the ingrate and the deceiver, to do the serpent's work amongst us like those Spanish anarchists and Russian syndicalists and all the other reds that hate our holy priests of God."

He took another short turn or two up and down the dais, this time with his hands behind his back, pain subduing anger

44

in his red and black visage. The pulsing in the Baron's neck was incredible. He surmised that the blood was refusing to go through to his head. Father Freshman faced the audience again, this time with his hands clasped in front of him.

"Most of you will have heard in your history classes or heard from your parents about Charles Stewart Parnell," he said. "Charles Stewart Parnell was a great leader of the Irish people, and he almost won for them national independence." He hesitated, as even in his state of shock the Baron could see, then took the plunge. "It is true that Parnell disappointed the Irish people in the end, but that is another story and our story is concerned with a moment in Parnell's life when in the eyes of the Irish people Parnell was all they had ever dreamed and wished for, a great Patriot who was about to lead them into the promised land of freedom. But as is always the case with great political leaders, great leaders of the human race, great men of all descriptions, there were those who would blacken his good name. There were wicked men, enemies of what he stood for, who wanted him destroyed." He held his clasped hands in front of him, frowning in serious concentration. Had he been aware, the Baron thought now, of narrative complexities, the difficulties of the story-teller's art? Did he see the contradictions and the explanations crowding in upon him? And did he decide, like others before and after him, to make short work of the Gordian knots?

"At this moment in Parnell's life, when the English leaders and the English people were coming round to the view that Ireland should be given her independence, what happened? A man came forward and he forged Parnell's name to a letter and he gave that letter to a great English newspaper, no less than the famous "Times" of London, the great Thunderer as it was called because of its editorials. And this letter and this forgery seemed to show that Parnell was implicated in a shocking crime, the crime of murder."

There was a rustle, of relief and of excitement. This was good stuff. And the majority were off the hook. The Baron stared immobile.

"Well the man was found out," said Father Freshman, raising his joined hands and making a sort of punching movement in the air. "Found out as all such plotters and deceivers are in the end, under the providence of God. And this man was about to be sent to gaol for what he had done. But such was the disgrace that his man felt and was made to feel by the people of Ireland whose leader he had tried to destroy that he stole away to an hotel bedroom in a lonely foreign city and there with his own hand took his own miserable and unwanted life."

He bent his head, raised the hands further till the knuckles rested against his forehead, and remained so a moment. Then letting his clasped hands fall again forward, he continued in a different tone.

"Well, that unhappy man was a widower, a man whose poor wife had already died, perhaps for all we know as a result of cruel treatment, beatings and vile insults, and he left behind him two little boys, friendless and unprotected orphans, orphans of the storm. Ay, and friendless and unprotected indeed they would have remained in the cold and cruel world, but for the Christian charity of a great priest and a great Irishman, Archbishop Walsh of Dublin. Archbishop Walsh of Dublin whose great heart flowed over with compassion for all human sufferings took pity on those little boys, sons though they were of someone who had tried to bring down and malign the leader of the Irish people. Archbishop Walsh of Dublin leaned down from his episcopal seat, and he used his great influence and he saw to it that these little boys were rescued and were sent to a good Irish Catholic school, the very same school that had recently been opened here by the founding fathers of this order. But he did more than that. He had the names of these boys changed so that no-one would ever know that they were the sons of the forger, so that they could grow up and go out into the world like normal people and be good Irishmen and good Catholics like anyone else. Well"—he paused here, hooked his thumbs in his girdle and faced his audience four square. "One of those boys was the father of one of the miscreants who were responsible for what we have been forced to witness in this college in the last twenty-four hours."

There was quite a sensation in the refectory at this point. Everybody turned round and looked at everybody else as if the

46

identity of the one who was the forger's grandson and the son of the charity boy would be miraculously revealed by a mark on the forehead or a sudden seizure. The Baron felt indeed as if his pallor—or was it a flush?—must mark him out, but he looked around with the rest of them.

"His own father was orphaned in awful circumstances," Father Freshman went on, "circumstances which might have shut him out even from ordinary charity. But that good and great Christian the Archbishop of Dublin adopted and befriended him; granted him the great boon which was given to all of us here, the boon of a gentlemanly Catholic education in this very school; and even, out of further forethought and kindness, permitted him a new start in life under an assumed name; his own name, the name of his wretchedly disgraced father, forgotten. The true identity of that boy was kept a dark secret ever afterwards by the fathers of this Order; but the time has come to tell one of those miscreants who created the disturbance in this house yesterday the truth, so that he may reflect on what has been done for him and what he and his father would have become without the fathers of this Order."

He paused, perhaps reflecting that there were too many fathers about for the good of his syntax.

"Yes," he said, leaning forward on the balls of his feet and working his lips carefully over the words, "a few truths, a few home truths, welcome or unwelcome, may be called for, and that miscreant will hear them. He will hear about his ancestry and his shame. And there are others who will hear from me in private. But the rest of you, who allowed yourselves to be misguided and misled like spineless weaklings and incorrigible cowards, you need perhaps to be told a few home truths also. About character,"—he punched the air with his joined hands—"and disloyalty"—he banged one fist into the palm of the other hand—"and disobedience"—he raised both his fists in the air and shook them. Then he let fall his hands, palms outward in the age-old orator's gesture of supplication, "and the spreading poison of disrespect for the ordained priests of our holy mother the church," he said simply.

And while he proceeded to deliver his home-truths the Baron, sitting quite still, was yet rocked with illuminations,

47

possibilities, certainties and terrors. He sat in the refectory cowering at the immobile centre of cataclysm, and although plunged by what he had heard, as everything seemed to plunge him when it struck, into a further depth of shame, his toppling world was nevertheless lit with flashes of a new clarity. The black box that he had found at home, his uncle's whisperings, his aunt's laments and prophecies, obscure feelings of his own, hitherto unreadable marks of destiny—all were suddenly illuminated and given a new sort of significance. He could not quite grasp what it was yet, but he knew how important it was going to be. Shame was the main emotion of course, but there was an odd feeling of dazzlement also and even a sort of elation. He could never really be like the others now.

That he was the one referred to he had no doubt whatever. And yet, strange to say, when later that day, after delivering himself of the home truths and the rest of his homiletic diatribe, Father Freshman called the Baron to his study for the dreaded confrontation, he made no mention whatever of orphans, archbishops, forgers, fathers or Parnell. Ingrates he spoke of at length and at leisure. Pride he discoursed on, temporal and spiritual, and arrogance beyond one's years. Slackers and stravagers, pedagogic and athletic, who had no *esprit de corps*, he inveighed against. Sloth, unhealthy habits mental and physical, the delusion that with one's limited capacities one could form one's own opinions, the danger of subjecting one's judgment to that of misguided newspapers and half-baked books instead of submitting to the wisdom of the priests and teachers, men of undoubted learning and experience who were set in charge of one, he assailed. The halfbaked notions that were to be picked up everywhere to-day from atheists, socialists, popular philosophers, journalists, Johnny-come-latelys, would-be G. B. Shaws and hurlers on the ditch, he spoke of as much in sorrow as in anger. The unspeakable excesses of certain factions, members of the Government of the Spanish Republic, he rehearsed again. He issued threats of a scarifying nature about the consequences of future misconduct. But he spoke not a word of grand-fathers, fathers (other than of the Order) or forgers of any description.

There were of course six or seven others who had been

48

marked out as leaders of the revolt by various spies and informers, and with them too Father Freshman had his private chat. The beatings that followed were exceptionally severe. From the first slaps with a pointer by a nun in Ballywhidder, (for not knowing the catechism, at about five) the Baron had been beaten regularly on the hands with leathers and canes and straps and sticks. This was the first time he had ever been beaten on the backside and it was after the President had handed him over to the Dean. The Dean had been the compromiser and placator of revolt. Like all of his ilk when restored and stabilised in power he laid it on with a savage hand. White terrors are usually more terrible than red.

The proceedings were solemn, painful and loquacious, but there was never any threat of exposure as the forger's grandson. Of course rumour was rife as to the identity of the one referred to in the President's harangue and it did seem to favour the Baron more than his fellow revolutionaries. Oddly enough, though, this did him no harm. In spite of their eager concentration on the President's words the thing was not clear to the majority: the rank of the historical villain, the nature of his offence, the circumstances surrounding it; these were obscure and rapidly became more so as tongues wagged. There were few or none learned enough to know about the matter offhand, and none skilful or energetic enough in the use of books to look it up.

One of the few that the Baron credited with any sort of understanding of the matter was Mr Johnny Fogarty, the present Minister for Justice, then the Baron's (to some extent) confidant and companion. And he never mentioned it. For the others all that remained was that the Baron was the grandson of somebody rather powerful and high-born who had done something wicked and pro-British a long time back. It was more or less accepted in time that he was the illegitimate grandson of some nobleman or great politician whose career had included a mysterious disgrace, possibly of a sexual nature; and this belief grew in acceptance as the Baron grew in seniority; the older boys, who might have had a slightly clearer impression of things, departed; and young newcomers were told about his origins and identity. In his final year he was an important and sought-after man, his earlier, minor disgraces—the nits, the Our Boys competition, the shit on his pants in the infirmary, forgotten or occluded by his glory. Such are the benefits of ancestry and a great name, even if nobody knows what it is.

On arrival in Dun Laoghaire he was face to face with his destiny again, as if the bloody thing ever let up. His destiny, in the shape of the box; and his destination, the out-house where he imagined it lying, lay to his left, towards the harbour and the sea, but he needed a drink. He had a felony to commit, a burglarious entry to make. One good thing about an imminent unpleasantness, he thought, is that it keeps all others at bay. He could have a single cosy drink, concentrating on the one simple, comparatively uncomplicated unpleasantness ahead. Accordingly he crossed the road to Mr Goodbye Ganavan's dark and peaceful pub.

On the side wall of the snug that he entered lay one of the Baron's favourite objects of contemplation: an oleograph presented to its subscribers by the *Sphere,* an illustrated weekly magazine, in the year 1916. The legend printed beneath the picture said "The Last General Absolution of the Munsters Before Le Bessee". A twilight scene in flat featureless country on a rather wet and dismal evening was represented, the last vestiges of sunset being still apparent in what was presumably the west. A mounted chaplain, his hand raised in blessing, his horse standing astride a cobbled road with glistening tramway lines, confronted ranks of kneeling, bareheaded men, a colour bearer with a furled flag balanced on one knee and three officers on horseback, their nags' heads drooping in the dismal damp evening.

The title suggested that the Munsters had got their comeuppins the following morning, and if this was historically the case the Baron certainly sympathised. A double ration of spirits perhaps? He rang the bell again, a trifle impatiently, and this time had the pleasure of Mr Ganavan's immediate attendance.

Mr Ganavan was a publican of the old school: white apron,

veiny cheeks and restless hands. Like many of his ilk he lived in a fog of misapprehension about his customers and their circumstances; and because the Baron had once in the moderately long ago been in the habit of visiting a girl who lived in these parts, Mr Ganavan believed him to have sojourned therein himself. Yes, he had moved. Ah, into the town, yes. He was, he was still at the painting. It was, it was a great thing to be at. Mr Ganavan often thought that the only true happiness in this world, apart of course from living a good life and being obedient to the commandments, was doing what you really wanted to do, what gave you satisfaction. He'd seen many a man you know plodding along and the only thing that would put a bit of life into him would be the welt of the stick. Those people were lucky who were able to do what they wanted to do and make a go of it at the same time. Of course there was no use leaving a family in want or anything like that to go off and do something harebrained, but if a man was good enough to make a decent competence out of something he wanted to do himself, surely there was nothing under the sun to equal that. Most of what was called advancement in this world was only people looking for power you knew. Power over others, that was what an awful lot of people were looking for, in business and politics and everything else, all of them wanting to order other people about, to give the orders and have them obeyed. It was a sort of sadism really. But nobody could say that about the artist. He didn't give orders to anybody, or take them from anybody either. He wasn't interested in that kind of thing. He pleased himself. He was keeping well? Mr Ganavan was glad to hear that. Good men were scarce. He went off into the interior to fetch the Baron's gin and ah Roses, yes, to be sure, and the Baron, relieved of his presence but immediately desolate, turned again to the morning paper, bought down by the Four Courts, which he discovered himself to be still clutching. In an hour or two he would have to face the ordeal of the first palsied search through the evening equivalents to see whether they had reported anything about his trial. Not that there had been much for them to report in the proceedings of the forenoon even if they had had a mind to report it. It would be different

51

when he was finally sentenced to six or eight years.

"Some in the convict's dreary cell have found a living tomb; and some unseen, unfriended fell within the dungeon's gloom," said a familiar voice.

The Baron looked up joyously. Riley stood in the doorway of the snug with his dissolute, banished emperor's head on one side and continued to recite:

"And though they sleep in dungeons deep, or flee, outlawed and banned; we love them yet, we can't forget the felons of our land."

"Chuck that," said the Baron. "It's too near the bone." He noted that his friend was wearing a rather smart, three button suit, guardsman's tie and striped shirt. Prosperous. "I know you've come to life again," he said, "but what on earth are you doing out here?"

"You forget," said Riley, "that I have connections with the Borough of Dun Laoghaire. Romantic connections."

"Ah yes," said the Baron. "Yes. The novelist's sister lives out here. On the seafront I believe. Everybody has romantic connections with the borough it would seem." He made a swift mental calculation. "Will you have a drink?" he asked as Mr Ganavan returned. But receiving Riley's acquiescence in a small scotch with an assenting beam, his hands performing strange ceremonies of ablution and benediction, Mr Ganavan continued his earlier discourse.

"I was just saying to our friend here don't you know that the only true satisfaction and happiness in this world, apart of course from living a decent life and receiving the blessed sacraments, is to follow your vocation whatever it may be: that is of course if it's consonant with the laws of God, I'm not talking about Hitler or anything like that now, but to do something that gives you satisfaction that's the thing now, that's the great and wonderful thing," said Mr Ganavan.

Almost unable to bear this on top of everything else and moved as well by some demon of mischief, the Baron said:

"My friend here knows all about that, Mr G. This is Patrick Riley the well known poet."

Mr Ganavan took Mr Riley's somewhat reluctant hand between two of his own, fondled, and, continuing to fondle

52

while he spoke, said:

"Well now is that the case? Is that so? I'm very fond of the poetry myself ... of course you have to have the time to read. And of course in the public house trade nowadays I'm afraid you don't have much of that. But I still remember a lot of poems from the old national school book, don't you know. Blind Caoch O'Leary, now, that's a very beautiful poem, or The Burial Of Old Sir John Moore after the Retreat from That Place in Spain, that's exquisite. You know we should be very grateful some of us that we had the poetry belted into us by the holy Christian Brothers because it's a great thing to remember afterwards. Of course when you're young you don't understand, don't understand at all, when you're a gossoon."

His eyes took on a misty look. He was still holding Patrick Riley's hand. From the cool, dark interior came a rough clearing of the throat, the noise of a coin being rapped on the counter and a plaintive voice: "Hey boss, anny chanst at all of gettin' a drink out here?"

Mr Ganavan released Mr Riley's by-now-quite-eager-to-escape hand, said "Excuse me a moment gentlemen please while I attend to a customer," and vanished out of the snug.

"I heard only the vaguest possible version of your troubles," said Riley after a pause. "From the incumbent arch-poet, who's now consenting to speak to me, so you needn't fear that the details are being bruited abroad in bar and brothel. What are they likely to be able to do to you? Is it really a question of durance vile?"

"It is I'm afraid."

"Jasus. Can't you cut your lucky?"

"Even supposing I wanted to they could probably bring me back. And Mulvaney has arranged a bailor whom I couldn't see stuck. So that's it."

"Well, forgive me for asking," said Riley. "I know what most people's concern must be like. And it's a good rule that unless you can do something to help you should keep your mouth shut about another man's troubles. Of course if he wants to talk about them himself it's a different matter ... ."

"I don't know," said the Baron. "I really don't know Paddy. It's so ... sordid. This time I feel really ... fucked up. Really

53

disgraced. In my own bones I mean."

"I'd be leery of that feeling if I were you," said Riley. "If I know you, you're probably the worst judge of that aspect of the matter. You probably brought yourself up pretty strictly, possibly with notions of honour derived from books and not from the world of—where was it?—Ballywhidder?"

"One possible definition of the moral hero," said the Baron, "is he who recognises the nature and gravity of his crime as more important than any man's opinion of it. Or him."

Riley looked at him sharply. "So that's what you're setting up shop as now? Some kind of guilt exemplar? Leave that to the writers for Jasus sake. How could you possibly judge the nature and gravity of the crime? You that committed it, an involved party? The man in the gap? I don't think you're thinking of the crime at all. I don't want to labour the point, but all us English-influenced public school heroes should watch out for the suffering caused by the notion of the self as hitherto honourable. Watch out for the daydream self. Think of poor Scott.

"Was it a very horrible crime qua crime?" asked Riley. "I mean did you really do something serious and irreparable to somebody's person or peace of mind or chance of happiness or power of achievement? That's all that counts, you know. And it probably doesn't count as much as you'd like to imagine."

"Latest reports suggest that the man I wronged and deceived lost his job on the head of it and subsequently his sanity," said the Baron.

"And you know that you're responsible for these losses? You're sure he wouldn't have lost them through some other agency if you hadn't come along? You make yourself sound like Genghis Khan or somebody. Here, you'd better have another drink. Which reminds me I haven't had mine yet anyway." He touched the little bell.

"Do you feel like telling me about it," he asked. "I mean, would it do you any good? I'm not curious otherwise."

"I don't know," said the Baron contemplatively. "Maybe. To submit the thing to your judgment. You'd be a pretty good court of enquiry as to the aspects of dishonour involved."

Riley laughed. "Being a disgraced man myself, I suppose I would," he said. "No fear of the bollocks I codded losing his sanity, though.Or his job either, considering he hasn't got one."

They both laughed. An apprentice came, Mr Ganavan being otherwise engaged, took the order and returned again.

"This should be mine," said the Baron.

"Oh let's not worry about that. I've got a few quid for once in a way. I've contracted to go to those benighted states again and they've sent me the fare to drink."

They sipped the new drinks, each with his own thoughts, in the cool of the snug, under the representation of the gallant Munsters.

"Well," said the Baron, "here goes. I don't quite know where to begin. It'll have to be a bit like the old books I'm afraid, two or three generations back. The fact is that I'm the grandson of a very distinguished man."

"Aha," said Riley. "So it's got to do with that, has it? A foreign minister of the third French Republic, according to the informed betting."

"That's interesting," said the Baron drily. "Not Irish at all. Splendid."

"No such luck, I'm afraid. He was Irish by descent. I've forgotten the name."

"Well good anyway. A wild goose. A nobleman. It'll be Leopold Marshal O'Donnell, Duke of Tetuan before they're done with it unless the truth should out," said the Baron. "But the truth is not too far from that either. You know it's a strange thing about ancestry, but you are never happy with any but your own. I have heard it whispered that I came from rich folk and I was annoyed to hear it. The little I've done has been done in the teeth of circumstance and it seemed to lessen my seriousness somehow to say that I came from moneyed people. And yet when I heard it conversely rumoured that I was an orphanage boy, some sort of whore's bastard brought up on public charity, I was annoyed also, though if that were the case it would make my achievement to date even more remarkable, my achievement to date being about six finished pictures of any worth and one unfinished one which has passed out of my possession."

Riley made a deprecatory movement with the drink in his hand. He did not know how serious his friend might be.

"And yet I always hated being orthodox middle-class, a fact which gave me some pleasure in my real ancestry when I found out about it. Whatever way we look at them social categories produce unsatisfactory feelings. The unorthodox is all."

"Indeed," said Riley.

"Of course when I was a child I thought we—Lord save us, 'we', even now—were middle-class in the Irish sense: petty bourgeois, Catholic, respectable, and even then obscurely I hated that. It seemed to me then, and has seemed to me since, that the middle-classes of Ireland were neither fish, flesh, fowl nor good red herring. Nor any other class of mammal, marsupial, bird, reptile or fish. Not even members of the brute creation I wouldn't say. The blood ran cold and thin somewhere along the line of their evolution."

"Were you never at a Bective Rugby club hop in your mis-spent youth?" asked Riley. "My fellow members of the middle-classes used to appall me in my salad days by their animality. But I interrupt."

"The ones that brought me up anyway were certainly not very warm-blooded, not very great lovers of what is often called 'life'," rejoined the ·Baron. "But of course maybe I am being intimidated as usual into believing that anybody else's lot were any different. You know what I mean. There is a certain class of roarer and shouter. The warm-hearted working class. The devil-may-care aristocrat. Literary schools, literary schools, with all that that implies in the way of studied response and concealment. Pretending that their forbears were big, smiling, ebullient, squandering ripsters. Free-handed galloping gamblers and all-inclusive embracers at the same time. Big mommas. Giant, drunken, poetically floothered daddas. Yiddisher mommas. Behanism. Blackguardism. Drunk every Saturday night. Life. But no sordidity. As if you can have one without the other."

He was silent for a moment, scowling at the partition in front of them.

"I can see that this is going to be a long story," said Riley contentedly. "So could we come to the beginning of it?"

"Anyway my lot were calculators and worriers," continued the Baron. "There was nothing rip-roaring about them except when the aunt was screaming abuse at the slaveys, whom she constantly accused of extravagance, dishonesty, impurity and other forms of fecklessness.

"You see I was brought up by an uncle and aunt, for I was, from an early age, what is called an orphan, a fate which, like any other, has both advantages and disadvantages. Brought up, as you correctly reminded us both a little while ago, in Ballywhidder, a hell hole if ever there was one, where my uncle was some sort of a customs man, in fact *the* customs and excise man. You know the miasma of ignorance about everything in which Irish children are or used to be reared. Well, in my case that included ignorance about my father and mother. I don't remember asking for very much information, but there was in any case remarkably little forthcoming—I mean it seems to me now remarkable, perhaps it did then too, but what I principally remember was a slight aura of a forbidden subject, a sense of—how shall I put it?—diffused disgrace. Oh, nothing that I was formally told could give me that, but it was there. The gist of what I was told was that my father had been killed in the first world war and that my mother had died of grief or something equally dispiriting and discouraging at round about the same time, perhaps even in giving birth to me, though I don't actually think they ever came right out and laid her death at my doorstep just like that.

"I further understood that my uncle was my mother's brother. Do you get that? He was my maternal uncle?"

Riley nodded, as sagely as possible.

"I only ever remember one set of grandparents. I mean one set is all I ever saw but no other set was ever even mentioned that I recollect and I don't remember asking about any either. I just sort of took it for granted, you know, that I had only one set: my uncle's parents, who were also my mother's. My father's parents, whoever they were, didn't come into the official picture. My lack of knowledge and I suppose lack of curiosity about them were complicated by the fact that the aunt's parents used to visit us too and I suppose in a vague sort of way I thought that they were my other grandparents, the second set that everybody is supposed to have, but of course they had nothing to do with me at all. The other lot, my uncle's parents—and therefore of course my mother's also—were small farmers who came from a place not far from Ballywhidder in the County Wexford. They weren't much—just pietistic peasants—and that side of my family hasn't troubled me much since. Well, as you know orphans are supposed to have all sorts of imaginings about their real parents. It may be that I am not very imaginative, not at all imaginative, but anyway I didn't have, and I don't seem to have had much curiosity in the ordinary sense either, but that is perhaps because from a quite early period all my curiosity became centred on one object: a sort of black metal box that was up in the attic among a lot of other old junk. I have seen other boxes like it since: black, metal boxes with a lock in front and handles at each end. I believe to tell you the truth that they were used to keep accounts and ledgers and things in. Maybe they were what are called deed boxes, but I conceived the notion somehow, perhaps because I had heard my father had been a soldier, that this one was what was called a dispatch box, although of course I had never seen any sort of an attested dispatch box either. It had my father's initials, R.P., neatly painted on the lid and I was as certain as anything that it was his and that it contained things that were of importance to me.

"For a long time in later childhood the thought of opening it used to come and go. I knew it would be terribly wrong to do so of course, for why else was the thing locked? Come to that, why else was it never mentioned? Nonetheless the thought that I could and would some day open it was a comforting one and I would often sit for quite long periods on winter evenings in the attic looking at the box and meditating on what might be inside it—swords, medals, letters to myself, money even, though the thought of proofs of ancestry beyond my father, I mean involving a grandfather, never occurred to me, ironic as it might seem. I suppose that box was the first object I ever contemplated with real intensity, and of course, as you know Paddy, it is in the contemplation of objects that is the beginnings of all wisdom."

Riley nodded. "Of course," he murmured.

"Well I suppose you have to go out into the big world to acquire any wickedness," the Baron continued, "and it wasn't till I had been sent away to Knockley College and come back from the holidays a few times that I decided to open it. It was a summer evening with the last rays of sun coming through the skylight and the summer street noises outside and I was crouched up there in the attic among my uncle's hockey sticks and pads, bundles of the "Missionary Annals" and "The Messenger" and the cabin trunk she had acquired the time she was supposed to go to America but didn't because she met him, and all the other junk that ever solaced them.

"I was always fairly handy with my hands and I'd done a bit of lock-picking at school for various reasons. I should have been able to get that box open in no time at all, but to tell you the God's honest my hands were trembling so badly that it took me ages. They were to tremble more in a little while and for a different reason, as you'll hear.

"The contents were in layers, separated by sheets of brown paper, and what was on the top layer wasn't much, or didn't anyway strike me as much at the time. There were a lot of old nineteenth century newspapers, copies of the Freeman's Journal for various dates in the eighteen eighties, weeklies which appeared to have flourished in the sixties and seventies with names like "The Flag of Ireland", "The Irish Debater" and "The Shamrock", scurrilous rags for the most part, a mixture of rhetoric, cantankerousness and personal abuse, often in the form of the most elaborately constructed innuendos, with a good deal of oily flattery of parties other than the ones abused thrown in. They were very much about battles long ago, but by and large they appeared to be of a radical, not to say violent, irridentist bent.

"There was also, in this top layer, a series of articles clipped out of the "St James's Gazette", which were signed "By An Old Fenian". There was a pamphlet, "Parnellism Unmasked" and there was a book, "The Memoirs of An Irish National Journalist". This was by Richard Pigott, of whom by then I had just about heard; but not much more.

"So far so uninformative, as I thought. The second layer proved more disturbing, and, even in the physical sense, more exciting. I was of tender years, my dear Paddy, easily aroused and easily shocked. What I found there both aroused and shocked me.

"First of all there was a packet, wrapped also in brown paper and tied with a legal string, you know—the red and white stuff—what's called red tape but isn't. I unwrapped it, fingers still trembling, but not as much as they were to do in a minute. It consisted of photographs, taken in the halcyon years of that art, printed in sepia, mounted, if you don't mind, on thick cardboard with embossed and decorated edges, and representing pretty young girls in various stages of undress being subjected to many and various forms of harassment and torture. Time shall not efface, Paddy, nor the years as they rise between conceal the memory.

"At a guess I would say these photographs belonged to the same era as the journals and were taken in the seventies and eighties. Subsequent deduction has led me to believe that this was in fact the case. Many of the girls therefore, those in a state of only partial undress, wore the undergarments of the era, the habiliments that must have been sweet mysteries to many a man. The erotic effect of these was more or less limited, though that is not always the case with representations of girls wearing underwear. Many others were utterly naked and it is noteworthy perhaps, or seemed to me later noteworthy, that though less elongated then the girls of to-day, they did not have that globular look we associate with the time, which in fact was due to the squashing up and squeezing out effect of the stays and corsets. Of course since this was the first time I had ever been exposed to girls in the flesh—or, rather, they to me—I was amazed at the girth of the upper thigh and the width of the pelvic region.

"Whoever collected the photographs or caused them to be taken or whatever had a catholic taste in forms of punishment and apparent anguish, but he seemed to have preferred that the poor dears should appear alone, or at least with the various and variously complicated engines and devices which hurt or tasked them, so that except in some cases where they were merely being whipped or goaded there were no men, and in these cases the men were masked. The photographs were about ten inches by eight and in some instances there were two or three copies of the same one. This, on reflection, suggested that the owner might have been a dealer as well as, or instead of being, a collector.

"In this layer there were also some books. I did not examine them too closely at the time, but I returned to them again and again subsequently in what I believe is called horrified fascination. You have doubtless, my dear Patrick, some acquaintance with Victorian pornography: indeed I see that some works similar to those I encountered are now being republished and even praised in intellectual circles for their literary merit and sociological value. You will therefore be aware of the crudity, the imaginative poverty, the repetitiveness of the genre. If the man who owned the photographs had an almost purist taste, in the case of the books he had to take what he could get, and that is never much. Those authors who catered to what, judging from the photographs, was his true bent, made up in violence of outrage what they lacked in subtlety of imagination, as indeed do most practitioners, even De Sade. Those whose obsessions were more orthodox were utterly lacking in descriptive powers and since they were concerned to an inordinate extent with one particular part of the anatomy, the cunt itself, their poverty was soon exposed by the limitations of their terminology.

"These books were printed on the continent, badly printed on poor paper which had turned almost brown, with French hooplas for conversation marks et cetera. Some were in two or even three volumes, for the Victorians brought the same fake energy to that kind of thing that they did to almost everything else. Whether the books, or, still more, the photographs, had any effect on my own sexual proclivities in so far as they diverge from what is laughably assumed to be the norm I cannot say. My probably reprehensible lack of curiosity about myself extends to many things about my own psychology. It's the manifestation not the cause that interests me. I am not even sure now whether it was the pain the poor dears were being subjected to, the positions they had been forced to take up, their nakedness or their beauty, for some of them were quite beautiful, that gave me the most pleasure. I know that I grew quite attached to some of them; but of course that doesn't mean that I did not rejoice also in the torments they were suffering."

"Of course not," said Riley.

The Baron paused for a moment in thought.

"And so to layer three, the first one to provide documents giving clues to the identity of an individual or individuals, though not in fact then very easily decipherable by me. There were great numbers of receipted hotel bills, ornately and solidly headed and evoking comfortable travel in Victorian Europe. They were made out to gentlemen of various names, some quite ordinary, Smith or Brown, others quite the contrary—Montmorency, De Vere, Arbuthnot, De Lacy are some of those that I remember, but the most frequently recurring name was R. or Ronald Posonby or Ponsonby—it appeared that the individual concerned used both forms."

"Aha," said Riley. And said again, "Ha-ha."

"The bills," continued the Baron, "covered a good part of the continent and intermittently the two or three years in the mid seventies of the last century. During this time the gentleman concerned—or to avoid argument let us say the group of gentlemen—moved about a lot, but he or they were fondest of London, Paris, Lyons and Lausanne. In London he or they stayed most often at the Sussex; in Paris at the Hotel Des Deux Mondes, in Lyons at the Bristol, and, in Lausanne at the Rambouillet. Besides the hotel bills there were those of various hatters, haberdashers, glovers and tailors. Not all of these latter bills were receipted, alas.

"There were also two bundles of letters or notes. One was made up of a series of brief, cryptic and repetitive communications. "Dear P. I am glad to hear you made progress with X and have made contact with Y. Yours truly E.H." one would go. And another: "Dear P. I hope X proves talkative and Y more so. Your E.H." Sometimes E.H. or E.C.H. as he often signed himself, sounded a little acerbacious. "Dear P.," he would say, "I fear we are not really making much progress. It is not at all clear from your last note whether you in fact succeeded in contacting a certain particular party or not, and if so what the value of the meeting was." There were occasional references to enclosures, "a draft drawn on the usual source" was the phrase used, and sometimes, I fear, complaints about "repeated requests for funds with little to show for the money". But there was also in this layer a flat red leather case or satchel, the sort of thing that was once used to contain note paper and writing materials. It was locked and after turning it over in my hands a few times I opened it simply by pulling on the lid or cover till the lock gave.

"I remember feeling as I turned it over that inside this there was going to be something specially significant, and I remember also fearing what I was going to find.

"What was there was another series of notes, as cryptic and as brief as the ones I had already read, but in this case signed P. and, sometimes, C.S.P.

"Not all were headed or dated. Those that were bore sometimes the simple superscription, London or Dublin. At least one said Kingstown and one Euston Station. Three however were on printed notepaper, headed Morrison's Hotel, Dublin; and one, Thomas's Hotel, Cannon Street, London, The dates, if any, were somewhat later than the dates on the bills.

"They referred almost entirely it seemed to financial transactions of some kind, but brief and cryptic though they were, they bore the imprint of a personality of power and directness. I have some of them by heart, more or less, and have had, since that first day in the attic almost. But remember that in the next two or three years I read them over and over again.

" "Utter nonsense," said one, dated from Morrison's Hotel, January 14 eighteen eighty one. "You ask too much and what you suggest is likely to prove an embarrassment rather than an asset". That was signed, "yours truly, C.S.P.". "I have your proposal," said another, which bore the superscription London and a date in eighteen eighty, "I would look upon it with the greater favour if you had proved willing to keep your part of the bargain up to now. However I will come half-way to meet you. P." There seemed to have been a protracted negotiation in eighteen eighty one. "I repeat that the price you ask is too high," a typical note began, "and I have clearly told you that the last offer was the highest I am prepared to make. You may take it or you may leave it, but if you do not take it you must look elsewhere for a purchaser for your property. Yours truly, C.S.P.".

"That wouldn't be the Chief by any chance?" asked Riley.

"It would," said the Baron somewhat grimly. "To the best of my knowledge and belief it certainly would."

"Holy smoke," said his friend. "Now we're trashing."

"We are," said the Baron, "but remember that nothing was clear to me at the time. I had been crouched up there in the attic for so long that the light was fading and I had had, you must remember, a series of shocks. And there were other things here in the last layer also. A child's woollen bonnet with strings, and an old envelope with tufts of auburn hair. A woman's undergarment of embroidered silk, what I believe was called a chemise. A photograph of two little boys in sailor suits on a swing. A photograph of a man in a first world war British private's uniform, who bore a definite resemblance to one of the boys on the swing and had my nose."

"Unmistakeable," said Riley. "And according to Napoleon a proof of genius."

"Indeed," said the Baron. "An 1879 edition of the Rubaiyat of Omar Khayam with a small crushed rose inside and the inscription "All, all my love, R.P."; a programme of the opera Ivanhoe by Sir Arthur Sullivan as given at the Royal Theatre Dublin in 1902 and autographed by the star Mr Joseph O'Mara; a bundle of letters from a woman called Philomena—that in fact was my mother's name—to a soldier at the front in the years 1916, 1917 and 1918, cold bloody letters it seemed to me, often containing reproaches about promotion and her circumstances as well as rather cursory expressions of love and eventually references to a baby that was coming. These came mostly from an address in Drumcondra and somebody, presumably the recipient, had tied them together with a purple ribbon.

"There were besides letters from various other hands, to me unidentifiable or unimportant. Two, however, were dated from France in 1916 and were signed T. M. K., initials that I subsequently deduced to be those of Thomas Kettle; two more were on the regimental notepaper of the Royal Munster Fusiliers and were signed W. Redmond, Captain, M.P. These referred to promotion to commissioned rank and the possibility of transfer. There were also three brief and rather uninformative letters dated variously from Paris in 1903, Trieste in 1905 and Rome in 1908 and signed respectively Jim, James Joyce and James A. Joyce."

"Well, hell open to sinners," gasped Riley.

In O'Turk's too the day was progressing and a somewhat larger company had now assembled, most of whom were making a good general recovery from their own terrors of the morning, whether circumstantial or alcohol-induced or both together. The short stretch of time from now to the holy hour held less to fear than almost any other time of day, and its conflicts, though sometimes lively enough, were more predictable. The first results from the three English meetings which were coming in served merely to confirm the suspicion that the correspondents of the morning papers knew less than they pretended; and the evening papers which had just arrived provided small impulses to friendly conversation rather than serious controversy. Refolded almost immediately and placed a certain number of inches away from the elbow, the paper was at least proof that some people in the outer world had troubles of a graver nature than had most of those present.

"Nothin' about a certain particular party in that paper anyway," said the pint drinker of the morning, folding his copy and putting it the regulation distance away on the bar beside him.

"Divil the bit," agreed the barman, who was polishing a glass. "He's not in dispatches."

"And who might that be, if it isn't any harm to ask?" asked a second customer. "Who's the villain of the piece?"

"A certain particular party well known to us all who sometimes sits not a hundred yards away from where you're sitting yourself."

"Arrah Jasus who is it?"

"The Baron," said the barman after an exchange of glances.

"Why is he supposed to be famous?" asked the other. "What's the fucker been up to now?"

There was silence, the air pregnant with enquiry.

"God damn it, give us the low down," demanded the enquirer, who sometimes spoke a modulated, partly self-created slang derived from the early talkies. "Give us the pay dirt. Give us the old flap doodle."

There was silence again, the parties weighing advantage.

"He's in trouble with the law," said the first customer.

"By the hokey man," said the second, momentarily surprised out of his Americanese. "D'ye tell me? What sort of a rap is he up on, wampum or women or what?"

There was a slight but disapproving rustle from a dark corner where the individual who that morning had been addressed as doctor sat hunched at a table, a *London Times* open and drooping between his knees, a ballon of brandy to his hand.

"Embezzlement or somethin' according to what we hear," said the first customer. "To do with a legacy or somethin' like that."

"You are wrong," said the brandy drinker. "Wrong."

"Well what then?" asked the first customer defensively.

"Uttering," said the one who had been addressed as a doctor, gazing into his *Times*.

"Uttering," repeated the first customer. "Uttering. What sort of beech la mar is that?"

"Uttering of documents," said his interlocutor. "Name of God, man, you know what that is."

All sat silent, pondering the phrase. None displayed ignorance.

"Where in hell did he get that name?" asked another member of the scattered company, perhaps to break the tension. "Is he some sort of a class of a parvenew aristocrat or what?"

The Times rustled again ominously. There was a perceptible coldness all round towards the enquiry. Authority

66

had indicated its disapproval.

The barman's mollificatory instincts prevailed, however. "Has it since I first met him anyway," he said, inspecting the shine on the glass he held.

"And that's not to-day nor yesterday," said the first customer in a flattering tone which suggested that some were more knowledgeable than others.

"All the same there is something mysterious about his ancestry," said the barman. "I mean it's not just a nickname. He was got under the blanket by somebody or other, some swell or other. That's how he got this monneker. I mean he may not be exactly entitled to the ermine but that's how the name grew up. Way back, when he was at school or something, it was found out."

"Well you never hear the fucker called anything else anyway," said the last enquirer, persisting in exposing the fact that he himself was a bit of a parvenew. "What the hell is his name? I mean his real name?"

"Sure everyone knows that," said the original speaker, betraying himself in his turn. "Doesn't he paint and all under it. Doesn't everyone know it. Ponsonby. Ronald Ponsonby."

The Times positively crackled. There was a prolonged, suspenseful silence. Then the barman's mollificatory instincts prevailed again. "Pigott," he said matter of factly. "That's his real surname. The other is a pseudonym. You know, a name he paints under."

The Times crackled again furiously. "Not his name," said the brandy drinker.

"What's that doctor?" asked the barman. "What did you say?"

"I said that's not his name. *The Times* tore slightly as the speaker violently changed pages. "Pigott. Not his name. Deed poll."

"What?"

"Deed poll. He adopted that name. By deed poll. Surely to God you've heard of deed poll?"

All were silent. The so-called doctor hoisted *The Times* and hawked behind it with finality, disapproval and contempt.

"Well what in hell was his name before that?"

No answer.

"I said what was his name before that, Doctor?"

"Ax me arse," said the one so addressed.

All tittered, then waited, non-plussed, condemned. Finally the barman, his mollificatory instincts prevailing once more, lifted his own paper off the biscuit tin where it lay and opened it wide.

"I see where it's denied now," he said. "About the swords of light. They were made in the CIE works in Inchicore."

The light seemed Autumnal. There was a dark concrete wall opposite the pub, topped with broken glass, and the afternoon sunlight which touched its upper part and glittered among the bottle fragments looked like that of Autumn. The Baron glanced upward. The sky was deep and luminous, lightly burdened with large dark-bellied clouds, their edges touched by a neutral glow, a pale, flat light. Autumn all right, and as he hated all involuntary evocations nowadays, he hated this one.

He thought of the wall he had to climb. Had there or had there not been glass? Could they have put glass there since? In any case he couldn't manage it. His wall-climbing days were done. If he were climbing over the wall to make off with Susan, now, that would be a different kettle of fish. Could she conceivably be there? Of course not. He knew bloody well she wasn't there. But as he stood at the edge of the pavement several scenarios of discovery and shame, with or without Susan, unfolded before him.

But he had something to do which could settle an issue of vital importance to him—and, somehow, even to her—for once and for all. He thought of his grandfather, who had played a part in deciding the destiny of nations. He thought of the chief and the chief's scorn for general opinion. He thought of Joyce in Zurich, daily disappearing into his masterpiece, and his father and Captain Willie at that same time in the trenches, fighting for the rights of small nations and homes fit for heroes to live in. He thought of the other contents of the box, unseen for so long: of the child's bonnet with strings and the woman's undergarment of embroidered silk. He felt a little stir of tender cruelty at the thought of the girls who had had to pose for the photographs so that his grandfather might gratify the simple urge to see pretty girls suffer felt by many, and presumably by himself. He thought of Susan, who was the kind-eyed agent of this re-discovery, and of her long brown hair and legs. He remembered Osgur, who would be rendered less ridiculous by the production of the box, and being rendered less ridiculous might even be restored to sanity. He thought of the gaol gates that would no longer yawn. And even though the jigs were starting up inside him like little engines, the Baron forced himself forward. Having communed with the Munsters, he understood the nature of courage.

But he had forgotten the ordeal of the dogs. He had been down the preliminary road of small concrete houses before, twice to visit and twice to reconnoitre, and each time he had been attacked by dogs. Now he could see three disporting themselves on the dirty concrete pavement of the roadway, and there were doubtless others in the rapaciously tended front gardens, piddling, scratching, puking perhaps—light, yellow, liquid dogs' puke—waiting for his advent. He stopped, the drink fading from his veins, its fragile, carefully nursed warmth giving way to an interior trembling. The dogs, the concrete roadway, the little houses brought it all back: the months of chronic hangover, the loneliness, the dodging, the depths to which he had sunk.

About fifteen yards down on his left, in the roadway, in the Autumn sun lay the dirty, white, mat-like, one-eyed sort of a fox terrier. A harmless animal, so far as he could judge. But were any of them harmless? Were not all dogs the guardians of respectability and therefore enemies of such as himself? And this one was a follower, a heel dogger, a sniffer of human nether parts, ruination for the nerves. Further down on the right, sitting up, privates on display, crooked forelegs planted on the ground, head cocked, already full of interest, was the ugly brute with the chaps who made a bronchial noise when he breathed and had been the bane of the Baron's previous forays. On the left again, rolling in ecstacy on his back, probably on shit or on a dead, plague-stricken mouse, was the other little terrier yoke that leaped and barked.

His progress down this hated stretch was usually a matter of wide zig-zags, crossings and re-crossings, as casual seeming as possible for fear he be thought a lunatic, or, worse still, a coward, by the eyes behind the curtains, the theory being, though, that it was possible to plot a course between whatever curs were about. To-day, however, he had a felony to commit in the neighbourhood and must at all costs not attract attention to himself. He would therefore chance the middle of the road and chance getting killed by a car.

The mat-like one got up as he came abreast of it and shambled over, wagging its scurvy stump of a tail, its one eye glittering. Oh God. Whatever its own intentions it would bring the others round him. The game was up.

"Go away," the Baron implored, as ingratiatingly as possible. "Good dog. Good, good doggy. For God's sake go away."

Thus encouraged, its eye bright, it gave a little happy halfleap with its forepaws towards his tweeds. The Baron almost broke into a trot, recollected the peril ahead, and stood quite still in the middle of the road, glaring into the eye. "GO AWAY" he shouted softly. Puzzled by this lack of warmth, the animal retreated a little, still wagging the tail, but diffidently now. The Baron went on, veering to the left to avoid the mastiff, bulldog, boxer, or whatever, which was now up off its haunches, its white belly and black private parts no longer an affront to common decency, but gazing at him, oh God, head on one side, black jowls drooping. The big bloody brute.

With the courage of those who went over the top because that was the way they were pointed, the Baron went on down the road, the mat-like one at his heels.

The dangers were now extreme. He must already be exuding that smell of fear that maddens and emboldens animals. He knew about this. Adrenalin. The release of adrenalin. But maybe he did not release adrenalin, after the past months, having none to offer. Well, if he did not release adrenalin, he released something else. The smell was invisible, not the word, to humans, but audible, not the word, to animals.

Not for the first time, not for the last, the Baron thought of the sword stick. Jab, jab. At the black slobbering chaps or chops. Into the pink mouth. Into the barrel chest. Swordstick. Ah the swordstick. But it was, too, like the water pistol full of ammonia or the red pepper for folk-singers and proletarian playwrights in the pubs on a Saturday night. If you were not the absolute victor at the first, drastic coup, you paid the penalty for having introduced such a note of savagery into the proceedings. Kicked to death in the alleyway. Christopher Marlowe.

Possibly not liking the smell of fear, the mat-like one turned back and left the Baron alone to encounter his arch enemy. Head down, hideously ugly, dull-eyed, it came at him while he jigged and skipped as casually as he could down the road.

"Get away, you blackguard," he said, "or I'll kick you in the fucking teeth."

The bulldog or mastiff slightly opened its chaps or chops and growled softly, bronchially, but with sickening menace, at him. He stood at bay, a lonely figure with his back to nothing, in peril of his life.

"He won't do you the slightest bit of harm," said a man's voice behind him. "He's only a pup. Sure he likes playing. Isn't that so, Jockser wockser? He wouldn't hurt nobody."

He opened a garden gate and the dog trotted peacefully in. The Baron's relief was great, but his rage now knew no bounds of reason. He cast aside all caution.

"Listen here to me my good man," he said. "You say that he would not do me the slightest bit of harm. But he has already done me considerable harm. He has released my adrenalin, if adrenalin it is."

The fellow looked almost hurt. "He was only being friendly," he said, aggrieved.

The Baron glared at him. "Assault," he said, "is a different thing from battery. No battery is needed for assault. If I walk down this road and you shake your fist at me, that is assault. I grant you there has been no actual battery but your dog has been guilty of assault. I wouldn't be surprised but that you yourself have been guilty of assault."

The fellow digested this for a second. Then he began to

open the gate. The dog bared its fangs. The Baron swung on his heel and made off as swiftly as he could, consonant with some dignity, listening backwards. He was not pursued, by beast or by man, and when the terrier thing came over towards him, yapping and leaping like a Liverpool poem, he swung his not inconsiderable legs at it in a sort of complex running kick which, continued, carried him round the corner where he knew from experience the dogs would not follow.

He had won a victory of sorts at last. But he was in no shape now for the other ordeal still to come.

"For God have mercy's sake, you don't mean to tell me," Riley had said, "but you bear his name. There's no question of illegitimate origins at all. You actually bear his name."

"I do," the Baron had replied, "and I am not illegitimately descended. Nonetheless I did not originally bear his name. As soon as I was in a position to do so I changed the name I bore to his."

"Bedad," said Riley. "Bravo."

"You see I don't think I was ever ashamed of him", continued the Baron. "Mind you, for the first few days after the business in Knockley College I was in a state of shock. Then I began to feel curiously delighted. For one thing, when I examined the contents of the box first I had had a sort of stupid idea that the photographs could have been my father's, and although they were already becoming a source of quite considerable delight to me, the thought gave me—well, it gave me pause. At that age, that kind of thing would."

Riley nodded.

"Maybe it wasn't so much the photographs as the books," continued the Baron.

"The books were a bit of a facer and it was a relief when I succeeded in surmising that they were only my wicked grandfather's. Still, over and above that kind of thing—far and away more important than anything like that—I had been given, as it seemed to me, an ancestry of great distinction. It may seem odd that I should feel this when the distinguished ancestor was in fact a blackmailer, a traitor, a perjurer, a forger, a false friend and a purchaser if not purveyor of pornography. Nevertheless, being descended from a man like Pigott who had played a distinguished part in history—and of course I was inclined to exaggerate the importance of the part he did play—seemed to make me a part of it, of history I mean. It seemed to connect me with history. I mean he was almost a statesman of a sort—somebody who had played a public part in things. It was better therefore than being descended from a nobody; and preferable too, it seemed to me, than having some undistinguished, titled landgrabber for an ancestor. I felt I had suddenly been put more than on a par with all the scions of our new political aristocracy who were my playmates at Knockley College, Mr Johnny Gogarty, the present Minister for Justice, included.

"And another thing which is maybe even harder to grasp is that what I now thought I knew—what in part I had discovered, and in part been told by the irate Father Freshman—seemed to confer a very genuine sort of distinction on myself. I felt I was famous, albeit secretly famous if you know what I mean, and that this fame, or this distinction, lifted me in some way out of the squalor that otherwise seemed to be my lot and that I hated more than anything else. Of course for years I had to take things on trust, knowing no more than I have just told you. Still, on the basis of that it wasn't too difficult for a fellow with a little historical knowledge—and I was always good at history—to work things out and arrive at the conclusions I arrived at: to decide that R. P. was Richard Pigott and P. or C. S. P. Parnell. Once I learned a bit about Pigott—and about Parnell—that was all clear to me. Adding the contents of the box to the story Father Freshman had told that morning in the refectory it became obvious. The R. P. of the box was Richard Pigott and he was my grandfather.

"Subsequent research only confirmed that what the priest said about the two little boys and the change of name was true, but I may as well tell you at this point what exactly it did reveal.

"You probably know a bit about Pigott. Everybody in Ireland does. Well you know that he forged some letters which appeared to show that Parnell was involved in the Phoenix Park murders. What you probably don't know, what most

73

people don't know, is that when he was forced to flee from the court proceedings which established that he was a forger, and not very early wise but still brave enough in season put the pistol to his head, he was a widower with two small boys to look after.

"He seems actually to have loved them—if, like the rest of us, only after his fashion—and he spent some of his few remaining hours on earth cadging and pleading on their behalf. He sent the Irish housekeeper who looked after them a cheque for the last five pounds he had in the bank. He borrowed, if that's the word, some more money from his solicitor, a fellow called Shannon, on the head of the boys' situation, and against all the apparent odds he did actually send the most of it to Dublin also. With whatever else he had in his pocket he then had a meal consisting of turtle soup, cod with oyster sauce and champagne; and he afterwards went to the Alhambra Music Hall where he picked up the sort of female he was in the habit of referring to as 'a pliant partner'. That phrase may have suggested unusual compliances and permissions sought and obtained or it may not. Anyway, they went back to her place, whatever that was, and we can only hope that he enjoyed himself and that she got as much as she expected. Speaking for myself, and also, if I may, on my father's behalf, I don't grudge it to her.

"Well, all that was on the Friday night, the night of the famous cross-examination by Sir Charles Russell which established that he had forged the letters. The following day, Saturday, he invaded the house of Henry Labouchere, who was an acquaintance, confessed the whole story of the letters transaction to him and George Augustus Sala who happened to be there; admitted that the game was up; and begged Labouchere to do something about the boys, who were now his main agony of mind and reason for his visit.

"Well, as you know, to use your own phrase, he cut his lucky. He was seen in Madrid three days later by, of all people, Captain O'Shea, drinking beer in a cafe incidentally, and holding up a newspaper with shaking hands. Dog doesn't eat dog they say, but it was O'Shea, himself of course a blackmailer, who informed the authorities."

"Good God," said Riley, "I didn't know that."

"Nobody does," said the Baron quietly, "except me. Well, anyway, after my grandfather, or perhaps I should still even say my presumed grandfather, for the proofs that have satisfied me might not satisfy the whole world, shot himself in the presence of the polite Spanish police, Labouchere remembered; and, whether he had promised anything or not, he must have felt some compassion, because he raised a fund for the boys in a weekly he ran called "Truth"—which incidentally lasted down to our own time."

"I know," said Riley. "I've contributed to it."

"It's a circular universe," said the Baron. "Anyway, the fund wasn't much of a success. The sins of the fathers you know, as I'll shortly be forced to recognise again. But the matter came to the notice of the great Archbishop Walsh of Dublin, who, with Labouchere's consent, took charge of the destinies of the poor little mites, orphans of a bloody storm they knew nothing about. He was a man of some decisiveness it seems, and, after he had got himself appointed as their legal guardian, he decided to do away with their identities and their disgraces all together. He changed their names; had them sent to a Catholic boarding school and brought up as if they were some other kind of orphan entirely."

"Well, words fail me," said Riley. "There must have been a lot of hugger mugger about all this."

"Oh God, yes," said the Baron. "Carriages, outfittings, midnight transferrings, suitable underwear, rosary beads, long pants and little man we've got a new name now you know, not to mention nuns and priests whispering in corners about His Grace's strict instructions. One way or another the job was accomplished and the secret was kept, officially known only to Archbishop Walsh, though as I have just told you I have evidence that the priests of the school to which they were sent were in on it too and with their long priestly memories they preserved it through more than one generation of little boys. Just in case it came in useful you know. The usual Irish clerical thing. The priests, as a matter of hard fact, know everything there is to be known about everybody in this country. I have no idea how much the boys themselves may have known or

75

remembered. I suppose they were told some yarn or other about the change of name, warned never to breathe a whisper about the previous identity, and gradually, as is the way with kids, got confused, or clean forgot, or invented some tradition, doubtless romantic and melodramatic, of their own.

"Anyway the little boys grew up and one of them at least, the younger, went in the fullness of time to the Catholic University, where he was the contemporary, and became the friend, of James Joyce."

"Holy Smoke," said Riley, "hence the notes in the box. Is he in Ellmann?"

"There's a lot," said the Baron darkly, "that's not in Ellmann."

He was silent for a moment, gazing into his raised Scotch. Then he lowered it in one determined gulp. "Push up another one there, Paddy, with some of that gold from beyond the seas. This is dry work. You're the first and only man I've ever told this part of the story to, let alone the soridities to come."

Riley finished his own, rang the bell and repeated the order.

"He got his arts degree," the Baron went on, "and became some sort of a civil servant, working, so far as I can gather, first in the Four Courts and then in the Castle—but I hope not as any sort of goddam policeman because there's enough disgrace in the family as it is without that. I have my suspicions, though, because he studied for the bar and apparently was let off in the afternoons to do so. In 1915 he was called to the same. I've checked up on these things. Well, the war was on and, as you know, Irishmen were flocking to the colours in their thousands. Apparently the only thing that had kept my hero father out of this titanic struggle for the rights of small nations up to now had been his putative barristership, for the moment he got it he joined up, and as an enlisted man too, mark you. Which he remained, as a lot of people did in that war, out of some sort of principle. Anyway to cut a long story short, in 1918, just shortly before the whole enormous shambles came to an end, he died—not, let us hope for king or emperor, but for a dream of something or other, born in Knockley College, and for the secret scriptures of the poor."

He lifted his glass for a moment towards the immobile

Munsters, then went on.

"But before he got his come uppins he got married—to a national school-teacher from the County Wexford whom he had met at a hop of some sort while home on leave in Dublin in 1917. Of that union, if I may so describe it, I believe myself to be the fruit."

He paused again. Riley was suitably silent.

"I know nothing much about her either as it happens," continued the Baron "for she apparently contracted post-war flu' round about the time of my otherwise safe delivery and died of it in the Coombe hospital. Let us do her the credit of believing that she may have been considerably shook by the news of his death, though one of the few things I do know about their relationship is that she had urged him repeatedly to apply for a commission both on financial and social grounds and that her letters on this score had taken on before the end a rather nasty tone, which up to his knees in mud and horror as he was, and likely at any moment to become part of the general filth, caused him acute distress.

"I'll skip the circumstances and the atmosphere of my upbringing if you don't mind, other than as they are germane to the matter we're talking about. I have already told you about the lack of communication between my guardians and myself on the subject of my father. Well, through my own choosing, it extended from this point on to the hitherto uncanvassed question of his ancestry. To cut a long story short, I kept the box and its contents a secret. For obvious reasons I did not advert to the strike in Knockley College; and being now quite satisfied in my own mind, and sure that if I asked them anything I would be confronted by blank denials or told a pack of lies, I kept my own boyish council.

"Anyway, time passed. I left Knockley, spent two years in U.C.D. doing architecture and then there was the second bloody war—our war as you might say, that I more or less ran away to. Funny, once upon a time we all rather liked wars because you could do that. Now you assert your independence by running the other way. Incidentally the first time that I ever used the name Pigott was when I joined up. Then after the war was over I stayed on in England, where at that time, believe it

77

or believe it not, I was very happy to be. It was really being in England that made the otherwise boring bloody war tolerable for me, and after the war there were the good years in Soho. I suppose that was the first time, old son, I ever found myself among my peers, people with whom I had a genuine temperamental affinity. They're getting harder to come by."

"Indeed they are," agreed his friend.

"Although there was no actual dramatic cutting off or reproaching I just never wrote to my uncle and aunt during that time. At first you just let it slide and then after three or four years or so it gets difficult. Besides, I'm sensitive, Paddy. Like yourself, I'm an escaper. Probably like yourself also I've suffered a lot of guilt about my vanishing tricks, but I think the people you have to vanish from ought to look to their laurels too. I mean if they insist on living lives which deeply afflict the sensiblility in every core of its poor being they can't really expect you to keep up a correspondence with them, still less to come and have tea and buns with them every Sunday.

"Anyway, all the time the box lay there—while I was in the war, afterwards when I was in London, when I was abroad—wherever I was. And in a way, the box was home. I don't mean that I felt I was in exile or any rot like that. I was thoroughly glad to be out of this place and I really loved England apart from being glad to be anywhere out of here. But I suppose everybody needs some connection with something and the box was my connection. The thought of it connected me up. Oh, I gave a lot of thought to the contents and I did, on and off, a lot of research, but the convictions I arrived at were associated with the image of the box. It was the patrimony. It was physical. It was my primary object. Sometimes when I was happy and working—I mean working in the way I did then—it seems to me that until lately I always went about it in the wrongest bloody way—the box would be my happy secret. When I was really happy, like in the London years with June, it was the big joke I had on everybody else. When things went wrong for me, when I had to leave her—or she me, for I don't honestly know which was the case—the box was somehow something to fall back on, what made me different and, in a way, what made me the same as everybody else, the two things

I've always wanted to be. And I didn't have to have possession of it. So long as I knew it was there I was fine. I was better off not having to tote it around with me from place to place. It belonged where it was, and where I discovered it.

"Well, about four years ago, Paddy, not long after I came back here the last time, the thought of the box underwent a transformation. Maybe, to mix a horrible metaphor, I ought to say that the fact of the box's existence took on a new dimension. For one thing I discovered they had moved. He had retired and they had sold up and bought a house in Dublin, here in Dun Laoghaire to be exact. A common thing with such semi-professional Irish country people when they finally jack in the job and discover they have neither friends nor interests in the hell-holes where they have spent their best years is to seek the larger community, I don't know why unless the presence of so many other people who don't belong anywhere either comforts them.

"Anyway I was panic-stricken at the thought, but for a long time I did nothing about it. Things were going badly for me as you know—how badly indeed perhaps only you know, old son. Frequently I didn't even have the bus fare into town from Terenure Road, let alone out to Dun Laoghaire again. When I got enough money to give me peace for a little while—usually only for a month or two—I stuck my head into the work, so that I wouldn't be thinking of what would happen when the money ran out. It wasn't bravery. It was escape. When I settled into Belgrave Road first I stayed there for two months and never went beyond Madigan's for a drink. That's when I was working on the picture you saw, the plank picture. Then one morning the money was gone and I took a bus into town and started floating round the pubs again. What the hell else could I do? I couldn't work; and even if I had been able to nobody would have wanted the bloody stuff. I couldn't rot or starve in the old shed, work or no work. At least if you're in a public place somebody might come by and make you drunk, so I used to sit in O'Turk's with Robert MacBryde who was in the same boat, God rest him, both of us more or less penniless, both of us trying to get drunk every day. This warm town as you know, Paddy, can be strangely cruel to a man in such circumstances.

The smart peasant, Paddy, hates poverty as he used to hate tuberculosis, and he particularly hates it in a superior man. He fears the contagion and he shuns the sufferer.

"Well, you know in those circumstances your judgement about people sometimes goes agley. You start frequenting the places where the drink is and associating with the people who will buy it. That's how I started going to O'Neill's, a place I would otherwise keep cordially out of, and took up with Osgur O'Bogadain and his wife. Do you know him by any chance?"

"I do," said Riley. "The compleat bollocks. A Gaeligoir. A regimer. Works in the Celtic Library."

"Did," said the Baron drily. "Well, you're aware that he's supposed to be a historian and that he wrote a monograph about Parnell. That was a sort of a bond in common," he said, smiling rather grimly. "But in any case you know what it's like when you're down. You meet new people who are enthusiastic for you when nobody else seems to be enthusiastic. Their circumstances maybe have a little glamour, or at least novelty, for you, so there's something of the ship-board acquainting about it. This fellow is a bollocks, as you say, but he owns a few books, he has a bit of apparently knowledgeable chat, and he's generous in a sort of way."

"And so well he might be," said Riley. "With the people's money."

"Be that as it may," said the Baron, "there was the free drink, the interested listener, the apparent respect, as if they thought they'd caught a prize in me, their misapprehensions—due to ignorance of fashion of course—he knows nothing about painting—about my position or reputation. And there was the lighted room with food and drink on the table and the night outside hostile and you penniless. There was too the wife, even more enthusiastic in her way. I don't have to tell you Paddy, surely to God."

"Indeed you do not," said Riley—somewhat grimly in his turn. "You don't have to tell me at all. About any of it."

"So I took to meeting him or them in O'Neill's and I took to going out there. Well you know how it is. You're inclined to adjust your chat to a man's speciality anyway, if it's interesting and he's putting up the drink. And I had my interest in the

80

period, what I might call my special knowledge of it. Besides when you're down, you do get a bit paranoiac. I mean you start talking about your war record or something equally abominable, your adventures in continental brothels, politics, the big bets you once had—anything but your work. Well, you know what I told you about the box giving me ancestral identity and distinction. And you see I couldn't talk about painting, neither to him nor to the wife, and I needed I'm afraid, or thought I needed, something exciting, something ... redemptive. Anyway, to cut a long story short, I told him about it, about the box, the circumstances of my discovery, who my ancestor was, everything, including even the Joyce letters, and historian as he was, he thought it all fitted in, said he'd do some research of his own and did.

"Now I swear to God, Paddy, the suggestion about the money came from him. I am not, as you know, no more than yourself, meticulous about money or where it comes from. In fact perhaps the reverse. And I did need the money, but I didn't go after the box nor do what I did eventually just because of it."

"What money?"

"Oh, he offered me money. On the library's behalf I mean. Said he could get the library to buy the stuff. So I went after it. But in any case I was desperately anxious to see it and handle it again, to prove to myself, if you like, that it had once existed. Do you understand that?"

"Of course I understand. It's axiomatic you would want to in the circumstances you were in. You weren't working. You must have been feeling the shadows of mortality closing round you. It was a question of clinging to your identity. Don't be teaching your grandmother to suck eggs. So you went after it."

"So I went after it. But there was another thing. I knew the game was up in Belgrave Road. I was way behind with the rent. I would have to leave and I would have no place to go. I wanted that bloody box to be reclaimed before they mutually conked out and their bits and pieces were dispersed, and I wanted it kept someplace safe, preferably in a bombproof place and at an even temperature and pressure. Of course I knew that getting it would be agony and that it would be sordid in the extreme, and as is usual with me when a thing is both sordid

81

and agonising, I made a hames of it.

"First of all I wrote. I won't attempt to describe the reply I got back. It was from her and it was all about what he had suffered from my ingratitude. Then I went out there. I saw him. I won't attempt to describe the interview. It was all about what she had suffered from my long silence. They had thought I was killed in the war, he alleged, and she had nearly died of grief, he said. He actually had the face to insinuate that my indifference might turn out to have shortened their lives. Anyway, though I got no encouragement, I went again; and this time I saw them both."

"Wait a minute," said Riley. "You're going too fast. I don't know anything about these people. I have no picture. Where did the interview take place?"

"The interview," said the Baron, "took place in the parlour, a heavily furnished room with many ikons, some of them familiar to me from childhood. There were the representations of suffering—the Christ and the madonna. There were the representations of joy—me in my first communion suit included. There were small tables with lace doilies on which stood plants in clay pots inside lacquered metal pots, floor rugs of red and blue cabbage designs on the purple and green carpet, a mantelpiece on which stood china shepherds and shepherdesses and an ormolu clock. I remembered as I say most of these images from my childhood and I reflected again while I looked at them what ferocious criminals most ordinary people must be, how strong and how near the surface the criminal instincts are, especially perhaps in the Irish."

"That's interesting," said Riley, "but how do you make it out from what you're telling me?"

"Well, you see, most of the objects and furnishings with which people surround themselves serve no other purpose than to prove what decent, God-fearing and above all respectable people they really are, and who but criminals would feel that need?"

"Fair enough," said Riley, "proceed."

"The images I was most affected by, however, were his hands clenched on his stick, the bloodless veins protruding, the knuckles showing white through the pale, age-freckled flesh, his stringed neck, her purple lips, for she actually wore lipstick, the mole on her chin and the three hairs on the mole agitating. I attribute to my profound distress before all these images, the fact that I actually broached the subject of the box at this second interview."

"And?"

"They denied all knowledge of it, said there had never been such an object in the house."

"Begorrah they did now, and what did you say to that?"

"Well, of course I accused them of lying. I told them all—well, not precisely all—about the box and its contents."

"Did you mention to them your suspicions about your ancestry?"

"I did, worse luck. Up to that point I had been referring to my father's box and as I say I had described the contents with some suppressions which were due to my delicacy and respect for their aged sensibilities."

"Doubtless, but when you gave vent to your ... suspicions how did they respond?"

"With bewilderment, astonishment, stupefaction, whether assumed or not I don't know. Eventually she began to make a dreadful sort of hooting noise. Then she had some sort of a fit and I left the house. I had little option."

"And have you been back?"

"I have not. They refuse communication with me in any shape or form. I can't say I blame them."

"So you didn't get the box. And as far as you're concerned it is as if it never was."

"Not quite. You see I know now it's there. But first let me tell you about the letter I got from them, or rather from him. This was a bit rambling as you might expect, considering his age. For a kick off there were about nine pages about how they had sheltered and fed and clothed and educated me when I was an orphan and nobody else would take me in. Then it went on to tell me that my father had similarly been an orphan, but that it was disgraceful that I should suggest that he had not been properly baptised and brought up. Of course I had never suggested anything of the kind. Or that he was in any way illegitimate. I had never suggested that either. There seems to have been an amount of misunderstanding rife during our emotional re-union. It went on to say that to cast aspersions on my own ancestry was a shocking thing and would undoubtedly be visited by the wrath of God. My father's father, my grandfather, had been, it reiterated, a decent, respectable God-fearing man, and a good Catholic whom I might very well take as an example in all things. The letter tacitly admitted that they knew very little else about him but that this should be enough for me.

"Then it came to the subject of the box. They said that they had had some property of my father's, including what they chose to call a tin trunk, with his initials on it. They said that long ago they had opened this and it contained 'nothing but a few odds and ends', so they had 'thrown it out'. They asked me to put 'all those filthy ideas' I had out of my mind. They exhorted me to prayer. They recommended especially St Jude. They enclosed some leaflets and a medal. They went back to the subject of all that they had done for me. They told me they didn't want to hear from me or see me ever again. They have since refused to answer the letters I have written them."

"You have written?"

"Oh yes. And my lawyers, if I may use that locution, have written to them also and received a reply from a firm of solicitors making many scurrilous charges against me and stating that currently their clients possess no property whatever of mine or of my father's, although they did once possess 'a receptacle containing merely some old newspapers and accounts of no value or interest'."

"I see," said Riley. "But in that case what about an tUasail O'Bogadain and the money?"

"Well, you know about the state I was in and I won't labour it. I suppose too at the end I really hated him. He would sit in O'Neill's talking about Ireland and the Gaelic. 'The problem of nationality', he would say, rolling the r as befitted the Gaeligoir, 'is a simple one. It's a question of identity'."

Riley laughed. "He could have said that again," he said.

"And I suppose at the end I hated the wife too. I don't know how I got into that. And then I couldn't get out of it. Once I took her, across the bed, with her clothes on, while he was in the house downstairs. I think I did it to shut her up."

Riley, suddenly serious again, shuddered. "You were in a low state, my dear fellow," he said gently. "I can understand." He finished his drink and pressed the bell. "Have another and tell me the rest," he said.

"Well, as I say, I had already told O'Bogadain about the stuff before I went out there to get it and he was all steamed up to purchase it for the library and had put whatever sort of evil bureaucratic machinery there was in motion. He had been giving me progress reports and telling me—briefing me, as he put it—about meetings and channels and I didn't stop him. I had let him go on and I had begun to think about the money as giving me a chance, maybe my last chance, but apart from anything else I felt now I had to prove to posterity somehow that the stuff had once existed. Funny thing is, I cared about posterity where this was concerned. More than I ever did where painting was."

"I can understand that too," said Riley.
"At this stage," the Baron continued, swallowing his lie, "I believed that my holy uncle and holy aunt had actually been deceived themselves and that they had thrown the stuff out all right, but by what you might call accident rather than design. It was gone for good, I thought, lost without trace. So I decided to recreate it."

"What?"
"Don't you see? I forged it."
"!!!"

"Oh it wasn't difficult. The chief's handwriting was like a precocious child's. You've seen Joyce's. E. H. didn't matter too much. Have you a piece of paper and a pen of any kind?" In silent wonder Riley produced an envelope and a pen and while he watched the Baron placed the envelope on a little table in the snug and inscribed some words, his tongue slightly projecting between his teeth.

My own darling Queenie
I have just received your
charming little letter, which [Tuesday]
makes my heart sing like
an Irish lark - You have
changed my whole life

"But," said Riley, "I didn't think there were any love letters involved."

"Oh, no. That's just an illustration."

"I hope you didn't put any in."

"Not likely. I knew the real letters by heart more or less. Of course I couldn't get hold of the actual hotel notepaper concerned, so I used what I could get in the way of old notepaper of any kind. Fortunately the chief was a most casual letter writer and used whatever came to hand. The letters from Captain Willie I used ordinary good old-fashioned bond for, the sort you can still buy. The receipted bills weren't essential, but eventually I substituted an old pocket account book I found in which I had my grandfather make the appropriate entries. I decided his handwriting was pure, old-fashioned copper-plate, anonymous and a little shaky. Joyce was easy. Cheap continental notepaper, the sort still used in rural parts, hasn't changed at all, and I got Paddy Collins to buy some in a village shop in France and send it to me. I'm afraid I made up for any deficiencies in the stuff I gave them by two extra Joyce's, one of them somewhat illuminating. They were the only things that weren't genuine so to speak."

"Indeed. And what about the photographs?"

"There's a fellow called Paddy Keaveny that I knew took photographs for one of those new English magazines that go in for women in their skin. A girl we were both acquainted with who drinks in the Bailey told me blushingly she sometimes posed for him. In confidence. Quite a nice girl as a matter of fact. Well, I worked round to the subject and he said that making plausible imitations of late Victorian photographic material was a simple matter. Then I told him what I wanted and promised him a bit of money. He said he could get a girl fairly cheap for what he insisted on calling S M provided there was no question of publication. Apparently the girls do worry a bit about the stuff being seen by their fathers and potential boy friends and to some extent that's what they're paid for. I explained that I wanted the S without the M and that these were going to be museum material only. We were in the historical forgery, not the porno business. Well, he obliged, after a fashion. I had to be content with a single model in various poses, none of them very interesting; and with machinery far less convincing than in the originals. Not convincing at all as a matter of fact. I will say for O'Bogadain's Gaeligoir ethic that he didn't seem to notice that this particular part of the goods didn't at all match up to the trade description. I don't think he notices much in that direction. Of course if Keaveny had let me direct the proceedings I would have made it more realistic, but he wouldn't. I was also hoping that the model would be the nice girl I knew from the Bailey, but no such luck. It was someone else he used, more tarty and not nearly as interesting to me. The mounts were easy. They still make very old-fashioned things for wedding photos and the like. I'm afraid I still owe Keaveny the money. It would have made too big a hole in what I got. He turned nasty for a while but fortunately he disappeared somewhere soon after, nobody seems to know where."

"How much did you get?"

"A miserable six hundred."

"Miserable indeed. Your grand-dad did rather better than that."

"I'll say he did. And of course he got his jaunts all round the place. Besides, mine was in many ways a more elaborate job than his and called for more versatility. The Parnell letters he allegedly forged were a simple matter, requiring little more than the signature. He appears to have had some talent for forgery, though, because he'd been doing bank bills and all sorts of other things for years. It's a talent I possess myself and so I suppose that there must be an element of hereditary skill involved. The trick, however, is to do things backwards. Start at the end of everything and work back."

"Like grandfather, like grandson. And this act of forgery is what you're in trouble for? It was found out?"

"O'Bogadain found a lot of things out I'm afraid, including about the wife, and he got quite vindictive and put the law on me."

"What did you say when enquiries started?"

"Well, I had a fit of concealment. I admitted the forgery part of it but I said everything I'd told him about my uncle and aunt or the box at home was a lie too. I allowed them to believe that my main motive was money. It was difficult to keep it up because the sergeant was a nice fellow and I felt like making a clean breast of it all more than once. The thought of the uncle and aunt being involved was fortunately so horrifying that I was able to resist. They assumed that the Pigott thing was a complete fiction on my part and showed no disposition to enquire into my actual ancestry at all."

"What is the precise nature of the charge?"

"Well there are several. But one of them is false pretences. Obtaining money under false pretences. I was going to plead guilty but MacNeice and Mulvaney wouldn't hear of it when eventually I told them the whole story, so I changed my tune and we reserved our defence."

"Well you'd certainly put a quare look on the false pretences part of it if you produced the real box in court and proved that you actually were Pigott's grandson. Can't you squeeze it out of them now that it's germane to legal proceedings—an exhibit in a criminal case?"

"Oh they don't know anything about legal proceedings. I wouldn't let Mulvaney do it that way."

"They may soon find out."

"They may."

"In which case they'll get a bigger shock."

"Well, I'll have to risk that, misplaced delicacy though it be."

"I suppose it's a pattern in family relationships. The bigger shock in return for the tender, temporary concealment."

"I suppose it is. Still, if I'm lucky they may never find out anything about legal proceedings or anything else. All they'll ever know will be that some time after I enquired for it the box suddenly went missing. You see I'm going to have a bash at getting it to-day, illegally."

"Are you indeed? But first how did you find out that it is there?"

"Well I met this girl—a girl who lives in the house."

"Great Scot. A slavey. Like the villain in a melodrama you've been making up to the slavey."

"No, no, nothing like that," said the Baron. "Nothing like that at all."

"I'm sorry. You sound a little cross. You'd better tell me about it. Go back to the beginning when you ... struck up the acquaintance. How long ago was it?"

"Well, I can't say exactly," said the Baron, though as a matter of fact he could. "I suppose about three or four weeks ago. She was just someone I met, just a girl."

"Just a bird you met somewhere and went lumbering down on in your usual bloody way?"

"Well, at the beginning yes. For a while, yes."

"Tell me the exact circumstance. You're an awful man for broad narrative strokes. You ignore the nuance."

"All right. I went to this exhibition of Paddy Collins's. She was with a fellow I knew and another girl. When I say I knew him I mean I knew him to see, but he knew me very well indeed, Christian name terms, how is old so and so getting along and all the rest of it. You know how it is."

It was Riley's turn to nod. "You had probably spent several thousand man hours drinking with him."

"Probably. He was red-haired, freckled, stoutish, cocky and affable. Could have been anything: journalist, accountant, television engineer, T.D. He had a Harold's Cross accent. He knew me very well. Insisted I should come for a drink. Wouldn't take no for an answer, and of course he had these two birds with him so I was nothing loth. At first I thought she was the one he was interested in, then I saw he was mixed up with the other bint. So I borrowed a couple of quid from him in the jakes and started in to enjoy myself. I never did find out his name or anything very much about him except that he knew John Jordan."

"Who doesn't?"

"Then we went to this party where there were some other people I actually did know. The party was O.K. I mean there was no messing, no bloody music, no dancing or anything like that. It was civilised and I could talk to this girl a bit and so I did."

He paused for a moment. Riley remained silent.

"Well, I didn't—what's the phrase?—get laying her or anything like that. In fact in the end she went off quite suddenly with this fellow and the other bint in his car. But it had gone O.K. I mean I hadn't got drunk. And I hadn't felt it incumbent on me to try to ... make her. Nor had I spent the night chatting her up only to find that she had slipped off with some Romeo who materialised out of nowhere at the last minute, faded on the crowing of the cock as you might say. It was just a nice civilised evening and I had found an intelligent, pretty girl I wanted to talk to and who apparently wanted to talk to me. And I had made a date with her. I went home in quite a glow. Woke up in one too."

He sipped his drink. Riley loooked at him tenderly. "You're coming on," he said. "Of course," the Baron continued, "this whole aspect of the matter changed when I found out who she was."

"When did you find out?"

"At the very next meeting. I found out first of all that she came from the country, from Ennis, County Clare. As a matter of fact she has a slight Clare accent. She works as some sort of telephonist or receptionist in a firm of accountants here in

Dublin, Kennedy Crowley I believe they're called, but her ambitions are or were theatrical and she is or has been on the fringes of the Baggot or the Focus or some of those. At some stage she was a student and at some other an au pair girl or such like on the continent. She has also been in England for a while. I suppose it's all a normal pattern nowadays. Anyway, in order to live in Dublin currently she stays with an aged grand aunt and uncle. Imagine my feelings when I found out where they lived and who they were."

"I can't," said Riley. "What were your feelings?"

"Indescribable," said the Baron.

"Did you tell her that you were a relative of hers?"

"I did not. I didn't tell her anything at all like that. But I saw the possibilities vis-a-vis the box straight away. They appeared to me to be almost heaven-sent."

"Perhaps they were. Do you know the precise degree of relationship?"

"Oh only very vaguely. I mean I can't enquire and I don't go in for that kind of thing much anyway, so I probably wouldn't be able to follow it. She'd be the daughter of a son or daughter of one of my uncle's—that is, also my mother's—sisters or brothers I suppose, whatever that makes us."

"Not exactly the forbidden degrees anyway."

"Certainly not."

"But when you found out how did you broach this business of a box to her?"

"Well, I told her I wanted a dispatch box like that to paint. Described it and told her it was very important to me and that I couldn't get one anywhere. I brought in Charlie Brady's painting of that hat box he pretended was Wolfe Tone's to explain what I meant. I went on about junk and its poetic associations for me."

"Phoney."

"I'm afraid so."

"But clever."

"Yes, it was. I asked her if by any chance there would be one like that in the attic or anywhere in the house where she stayed. I said there often were in old people's houses."

"And?"

"She agreed to look and told me there wasn't. She described all the other contents of the attic and I remembered it all correctly. Even though it's a different house it has an attic and the same stuff is up there."

"But no box."

"No box. Then apparently she had occasion to visit this outhouse at the bottom of the garden. She wanted someplace to put a bike she wasn't using out of the rain or something like that. There was a lot of other junk there. She poked about a bit and found the box. It was the box all right. No doubt about that. R.P painted on it and everything else."

"Well, well. And did you ask her to borrow it for you?"

"I did. She refused. But between jest and earnest, you know how it is, she told me they were going away yesterday for a while so she would have the house to herself and I have decided to get over the garden wall and have a bash at getting the box while she is out at work to-day."

"When did she give you this information?"

"Two or three days ago."

"And this was after you had been seeing her for—how long did you say?"

"About three weeks."

"And all that time you were ... making up to her?"

"Well, yes."

"And she knew nothing about your identity?"

"No."

"Nor about your interest in any particular box?"

"No."

"And were you making—how shall I put it?—demonstrations of affection? Protestations?"

"The day for that kind of thing is nearly gone I'm afraid."

"But you allowed the girl to think you were fond of her for her own sake, at the very least to think that you desired her company. Desired her in the other sense too perhaps?"

"Yes but you see I am fond of her. I do desire her. At least I think I do. To tell you the God's honest, Paddy, my feelings at this stage are so mixed up that I don't know what I want. I think I want to fuck her to-night after I get the box. She's quite a dish. In any other circumstances she'd be a godsend. I mean on her own, box or no box."

"You haven't fucked her yet?"

"I have not."

"Does she?"

"I don't know."

"If she does, I mean if she's that kind of girl, it's a wonder you've been able to keep her in tow without."

"From my point of view or hers?"

"Oh hers, of course. If she's that kind of girl. Your chase had other than a beast in view. You're a clever fellow, though, to manage it without fucking her. That's if she's that kind of girl. Why didn't you have a go? You might as well have had it both ways."

"Oh come off it, Paddy. You know better than that."

"Yes, well I know you. Let's leave it that way. One more thing. Are you sure she knows nothing, suspects nothing about the relationship, forbidden degrees or not?"

"Of course I am. How could she?"

"Well she could have said something to the aunt and uncle about this painter chap she had met."

"Ponsonby? That would mean damn all to them. They don't even know I am a painter."

"Of course. Well it seems to me that you have had a turn of luck. That this girl, dish or no dish, has given you a bloody great break, the required opening on the rails in fact. The next step of course is to get over the wall and get that damn box."

"I am going to do that right now as soon as we finish this drink," replied the Baron. "That is why I trekked out here this morning to the royal and ancient borough of Dun Laoghaire."

"And the best of British, Roddy, that's all I can say. Can I be of any help?"

The Baron thought for a moment. "No," he said. "I'll go this one alone. But listen—I'm meeting her this evening and I'll bring her along to Dwyers about half past eight. I'm to ring Mulvaney to tell him how I got on, and I might ask him to come along there too. In a way it'll be a little celebration, though she won't know that. He wants to meet her anyway, just to cast an eye, you know."

"And so do I, old son. So do I," said Riley.

"It's worth the casting I'll tell you that," replied the Baron, putting down his empty glass.

"Just so long as she's not one of those fragile blue-eyed blondes that you sadists are so fond of," said Riley, glancing sidewards at his companion. "Bloody man-eaters they are."

After leaning against a green garden railing to recover, he continued along the terrace of large gloomy houses, the sea on his right, areas of blue, areas of green and the grey slab of the harbour. Little yachts danced on the enclosed water, masts and spars describing lateral and vertical arcs, occasional full ovals, forward and reverse, above hulls of uneasy intersecting curves. Far out towards Howth four irregular white triangles trailed by white rhomboids pitched forward, paused, jerked back irregularly. It was a subject which appealed to one of his baser instincts, a love of boats and the sea. It had the attraction of mere poetry, and accordingly he hated it. As for the far smudge of the North Wall with its oil tanks, chimneys and gantries distantly, delicately visible as flat dark outlines in their own haze, Monet could have it. He could have the whole damn lot for the matter of that. And had, for the matter of that. Poetry. But at least it was heavy, lazy summer again over there.

About half-way down the terrace, and mercifully before he came to the one he had to burgle, there was a break between the houses where a short lane led to another lane or carriageway behind. He turned into this and then into the second lane which was flanked on either side by garden walls. There was nobody about. Of course he was overlooked by the rear of the houses on either side, but he had to risk observation of this sort. The thing had to be done and he would probably only be seen if at all as he crossed the top of the wall.

He went on down the lane until he came to where the telephone pole stood, a foot or two out from the wall and with wire guys running down from above on either side of it. He reached up and grasped a wire with both hands, then flung his feet up and sideways, his toes scrabbling at the wall for a hold and dislodging small lumps of plaster. No good. He released his grip on the wire and stood back in the lane a bit to assess the situation.

He began to pick out footholds, places where the plaster between the stones had fallen away and there was a large fissure. Keeping his eyes on the first two or three of them, he reached up over his head and grasped the wire again. Leaning slightly sideways, he raised the right foot and put it on the first of his ordained little ledges. No use. It would be difficult without a twist beyond his powers to get the left toe-piece into the next ordained fissure and thereafter he would be dependent on the left leg, notoriously weak since Hamburg, for balance and leverage. Left first then, and so, after a return to ground, he put the tip of his left shoe into the first fissure. Good. Cautiously, dependent more now on the grip of his hands on the guy, he raised the right foot from the ground and put it in its turn into its foremarked crevice. Excellent. He got the left foot out from under, then over and into another crevice. Then hurriedly the right again.

His face was altogether too close to the wall, but he could see his feet and where to put them. He got his left foot out from under the right and moved it up again. It found the crevice, but it seemed by no means secure. He was convinced that if he moved the right foot would slip. So he clung on as he was for a while, like a sort of spider, terrified and exhausted, yet somehow, merely because he was no longer moving, at peace.

Then behind him, on the ground, he heard a sort of snuffling, snot-breathing noise and a sort of liquid bronchial bubbling. Full of dreadful foreboding, his heart pounding, he twisted his head to look down and backwards under his arm.

Jockser wockser stood beneath him, forefeet splayed out, head malevolently raised so that his hooked teeth, pink tongue and serrated, black, gutta percha seeming inner fringe of the jaw were all on view ... . The brute padded a little closer, raised his head further and rasped out a growl through the bronchial bubble. The Baron was treed.

He wanted to take his eyes away from the teeth and the gutta percha fringe but the paralysed one now was the human being. Captain Marryat be damned. As he watched, the brute's black orbs moved, showing red at the corners. The weakness of fear flowed through the Baron's limbs. Would he even be able to hold on? He felt his toes slipping and desperately pressed them in. The wire bulged accordingly out. He seemed to be swaying. He dared not move.

He was forced into terrified action eventually, as proud spirits often are, by the fear of human ridicule, that blessed fear which is so often greater than any other. Three little boys had materialised in the lane and begun excitedly to profer advice.

"Mind yerself mister, that oul wire is goin' to snap," they said gleefully.

"Stay where ye are or the bowler'll ate ye," they warned.

"Go on mister, throw yer leg over it there. Es ony a weenchy bit more," they exhorted.

Then they began encouraging the dog to heavy frenzy by dancing and pointing. The Baron made his effort almost unconsciously, hand over hand on the wire, feet scrabbling precariously against the stones and mortar, the brute dancing beneath him, growling and bubbling like a canine volcano, the children cheering him on.

As one foot gave way in a small shower of mortar he got the other one over and gripped hard with the back of his leg.

He hauled and pushed himself further over. He was now lying in a twisted but horizontal position, his legs almost astride the wall, the upper part of his body some distance out from it, still supported by the wire. Though his trunk still faced the wall he was just able to look down at his enemies, the dog making ungainly leaps with its great mouth open towards him, the children doubling themselves up, hands on hips, to show extremes of mirth.

"Jasus he's spread-eagled," they said.

"Mind yer mickey mister," they cried. "Them stones ed catch ye awful sharp."

"Let go o' the wire mister, the pole is comin' down."

The dog padded to and fro, raising his bulk against the wall occasionally, a noise like a lead foundry coming from his gullet.

With a great effort of will the Baron removed his right hand from the wire and grabbed at the top of the wall. Dizzy and sick as he was, he succeeded in keeping his balance, and now could remove the other hand also, so that eventually he sat astride the wall with his two sweating hands on top of it. The urchins, if that was what they were properly called, raised a cheer.

Safe on top, possessed of a rash fury, he began to tear bits of stone and mortar off the wall and to hurl them down at Jockser. The children scattered to the far side of the lane and returned a fusillade of clods and pebbles. He abandoned all thought of retaliation. It was essential to get down off this wall. He might be seen from the neighbouring houses. He prepared to drop.

There were, he knew from experience, two ways of getting off a wall, both unpleasant and both dangerous. You could sit on top and begin to lower yourself forward while keeping your hands on the wall behind you, then spring outward and attempt to keep your balance in landing. Or you could turn around, cling by your hands with your face to the wall, lower yourself as far as possible and then let go backwards, into the void.

A sod went by his ear, spattering his face, so that he got the taste of earth in his mouth and the smell in his nostrils. He chose the turning round method. Scraping his knees badly in the process he succeeded in lowering himself until he hung by the length of his arms. The drop should now be no more than two or three feet. He let go.

He was at first unable to pick himself up. Forced to thrust himself away from the wall to avoid further scraping, he had landed in a sort of backward run and tripped over his own heels. He sat now on the ground at the point where he had eventually come to rest, a considerable distance out from the wall. He had difficulty in getting his breath and he didn't give a damn whether he was seen by the neighbours or not. He was too distressed.

Then he saw the outhouse of which Susan had spoken. It was a real beauty, a large, stone-built, slate-roofed structure with a door in the middle and two wooden framed windows. There was even a large sky-light and the first thing that struck the Baron about the whole affair was what an admirable studio it would make.

He picked himself up and approached it. It stood with its

97

back to the neighbouring garden and the end-walls were blank, so only the front offered entrance. The windows were proper windows divided into four panes, but the frame in each case was single and in the Baron's judgement they had never been meant to open. He could see heavy cobwebs inside. The door was a solid, wooden affair, with a handle and even a latch, but it was locked for all that. He could, he supposed, smash one of the windows, breaking the wood of the frames as well as the glass, but something in his nature revolted against that. It would have to be the door.

The way to open a locked door is to stand against the opposite wall of the hotel corridor and hurl yourself against it, shoulder first. That is the way the detectives do it in the pictures, but the Baron could not emulate them since he was not in a hotel corridor. The best he could do was to take a little sideways run and hit the locked side hard with his shoulder. The trouble was that the projecting part of the latch would have given him a wound in the shoulder if he hurled himself directly against it, so he had to avoid it by a small but at the same time debilitating margin, and it was only after a number of runs that he began to feel something give. When he did, he didn't like it. The splintering he heard and the movement he felt suggested that he was doing the wrong kind of damage. It was the hinges on the other side that were giving as much as the lock. He didn't want to smash this old door down entirely and so he altered his tactics and began to kick at the lock itself with a ponderous heel. He was hoping that the staple of the lock itself would give, and eventually it did, though to his distress only by considerable splintering of the jamb.

He knew immediately that the box was not inside. There was a girl's bicycle. That would be Susan's, he supposed, and he laid his hand lightly on the saddle with a mixture of emotions. There was a lawn-mower and an ordinary cabin trunk and there were two or three old dining-room chairs. But there was no box.

The place was every bit as commodious as he had supposed from the outside and the objects it contained were disposed over the floor with plenty of space between and around them. It was obvious though that there was no box and that there could be no mistake. Just in case, he tried the lid of the trunk. It lifted, but the thing was empty. Either Susan was lying or the box had since been shifted.

After a few desolate moments he emerged again into the garden. He looked towards the house, the windows of which appeared to be looking at him. He would have to break and enter again. He was now in a very advanced stage of the jigs, almost in the d.t.'s in fact, but he would still have to do it. It was not for nothing that the Baron had communed more than once with the Munsters.

She was standing with her back to him outside Doheny and Nesbitt's, wearing a very short brown dress, her weight on one projecting hip, a stance that only girls can adopt. The dress was slightly rucked over the projecting hip and a suede jacket hung by a finger tip over one shoulder. She was waiting for him outside the pub for some reason, the foot at the end of her lovely non weight-bearing leg describing impatient half circles on its high heel. He felt a stir of lechery mingled with his other feelings, whatever his other feelings were.

As he approached she turned her face partly sideways towards the opposite side of the street and he could then see her profile, the firm jawline softened by the small underswelling of the chin that to the Baron, rightly or wrongly, suggested reserves of sensuality. Her shoulder length brown hair was lustrous in the evening sunlight.

Suddenly her stance dissolved. She turned right around to face towards him, gave a little half wave with her free hand, took a step or two forward and then stood in that position of relaxed expectancy that only girls can manage, her head a fraction lowered, eyes brown under well-marked brows and bang. She was smiling. He suddenly knew that she was in fact very pleased to see him. Rage stirred in him also.

"Let's go over to this other place," she said, gesturing with the free hand towards Toner's. "I didn't want to go in there. I have something to ask you."

They sat at a table in the corner. It was a rule with the Baron, as with some other doomed men, to put off his

99

perplexities in the presence of attractive women. Besides which a little lightness and non-insistence of demeanour was, up to a point, essential if he was going to have his way of her to-night.

But it wasn't easy. He had just suffered a severe blow when his hopes had been raised very high. And he couldn't tell her anything about it.

"You didn't ring me up," she said. "You said you would. I didn't know whether we were supposed to meet or not."

"Oh, I've been having a hell of a time of it," he replied. "Agonies beyond count or compare." This was the wrong line of chat, blast him. Up to a point he was supposed to be the distinguished master of a mysterious life-style.

"Listen." she said. "You know Tim Halloran?"

He didn't. He shook his head.

"Of course you do," she said. "That was how we met. You know him well."

Oh, that fellow. How dare she assume he knew him? This girl had a lot to learn. "Yes," he said. "Of course. I'm sorry. I wasn't thinking."

"Well, I met him to-day," she said. "He told me you were in some sort of trouble."

Oh God!

"Are you?" she asked.

The Baron looked into her concerned eyes. The game was up. Sordidity was waiting to engulf him and there was no box or papers to give the thing dignity. This girl's acquaintance was about all that remained of the whole box business now. In a way it would be nice to tell her the entire story. Her eyes were brown highland tarns, flecked with a northern light. Her hair lay partly over her thin shoulders, some loose ends curled in towards the throat. He would fuck her to-night. He would have one good, night-long stretch of usage and abusage, something to remember them all by, his grand-da and Captain Willie and the lot.

He looked directly at her, his expression grave, troubled and frank.

"I don't know how he knows," he said, "and I wouldn't call it trouble exactly. There's an element of danger of a sort"—here he raised his hand to prevent her speaking—"and

100

I'm sworn to secrecy, so I can't tell you very much. I'll tell you the lot when it's over." He looked deliberately round the pub, then faced her again. "It's political," he said. "I have certain contacts and I'm acting as a sort of go-between."

Susan looked at him dubiously. "Oh all right," she said. "Have it your own way. But take care."

The drink he had ordered came and the Baron paid out a little of the money he had got from Riley.

"Listen," she said. "Before I forget. Remember that box you asked me about?"

The Baron, controlling his eagerness, nodded deliberately.

"Well," Susan said. "It isn't there any longer. In the shed. It's gone. And there's another thing. Somebody got over the wall and smashed in the door of that shed. At least I think they must have got over the wall. The funny thing is that they didn't take anything except the box—if they took the box. Anyway the box is gone."

"That's a pity," the Baron heard himself say.

"But why should anybody want a box like that?" asked Susan.

"I suppose it was just blackguardism," said the Baron. "Young shavers with nothing else to do."

"It's strange, though," said Susan, "because they smashed in the back door of the house as well, but they don't seem to have taken anything from there either, don't even seem to have come in."

"They probably got a fright at that stage," said the Baron grimly.

They all walked down to O'Turk's in the summer evening, along the Green, under the trees. A light rain had fallen, laying the dust, creating earth and leaf smells. Susan walked in front with Riley, Mulvaney and the rest, her suede jacket draped over her shoulders, her beautiful legs pale in the passing lamplight. Their laughter floated back to where the Baron walked with MacNeice, her's making a full, clear diapason with the others.

"Well, in my opinion, that would appear to be that," said

MacNeice. "There are forms of compulsion that we could adopt or the court adopt in relation to the present charges to make them produce the stuff and even testify to it supposing they still had it, but you've ruled them out; and in any case I'm now inclined to doubt very much if they do any longer have it. My own view is that it was all thrown out long ago whether by accident or design and that the girl is somehow mistaken in saying she ever saw such a box. Incidentally, the material that you gave O'Bogadain and which now can't be found was still in the custody of the Celtic Library, in O'Bogadain's custody in fact, when it disappeared. It wouldn't pass into the custody of the police until after it was produced in court. As you know they're in a very disorganised state in the Library. They say they haven't enough space and no funds for cataloguing, and with him locked up it may be difficult to find. That's our hope now—that it has vanished as well. But we'll have to face them on Monday just the same. And if you don't mind my saying so as a friend," he continued, "it behoves you to think a bit about things in general, however this business turns out. Even if you don't go to gaol—which, let us devoutly hope, you won't—you should perhaps give some thought to what you are going to do. Circumstantially speaking, I mean."

He gazed ahead into the midsummer darkness, his face impassive, a heavy mask of sensual content. "Has that girl any money?" he asked.

"I don't think so," said the Baron. "I don't really know."

"What are her circumstances? Is she married? Has she been? What does she do?"

"She has never been married, so far as I know," answered the Baron. "She works in an office. She has appeared on the stage. She may still have theatrical ambitions, worse luck."

"She's an attractive thing," said MacNeice. "Early twenties. Agile. Fun. Is she your girl? Is she going to be?"

He got no answer but he voiced his thoughts. The dew drop on the rose. Lovely. But at the same time the Baron should watch his step. In his opinion there were very few successfully consummated and happily concluded fancyings in this sad world. Nearly every fully explored sexual encounter between equal and intelligent human beings began a relationship of some kind, one which became semi-domestic and curiously permanent before you knew where you were or had calculated the consequences, unless in fact there was an airline ticket in one or other party's wallet or bag to begin with. There were of course amateurs of variety, but no matter what was said about permissiveness, you didn't get much that was memorable from them. And in any case they often turned out not to be amateurs of variety at all. Quite the contrary in fact. They were usually merely fucking out of some sort of anxiety. Neurotics in fact, though they might want you to believe that it was physical and that it was your prick they wanted. Sad. Societal partly, but had much more to do with the nature of women. Mind you the really transient and happily fleeting thing was commoner among homosexuals, but in that large and respectable body the transient thing usually had a commercial basis, concealed or otherwise.

"And," he added sourly, "it's seldom that transient either."

"When I was a young man," he continued harshly, "I used to stay with Sir George Murphy out in Ardash quite a lot. It was a great house for people to come out to. There was always a party going on. It was in the country, but near enough to town, and it was a good ploy for seduction purposes to suggest a visit to your noble friend. Poor old George was hospitality itself and of course he had a big house with lots of bedrooms and bathrooms. He was very progressive in his views—very much in reaction against his own background and religion and the priests and that kind of thing—and his progressivism included the encouragement of sex of all descriptions, including adultery, homosexuality and combinations of both. Well, I was a rather provincial young fellow and I didn't as I thought know how to go about things, or how to assess the consequences. Accordingly I often made the mistake of envying my more sophisticated acquaintances, seeing what I thought were happy little attractions happily, lightly managed to the point of sensual peace. Divil the bit of it. Most of them have been fighting it out ever since, in sickness and in health. I'm litigating for some of them at the moment, mensa et thoro, custody of children, divisions of property, damages for personal injury. And that's nigh on twenty years ago I'm talking about."

They crossed the road and went on down Grafton Street through the summer strollers.

"The Duffy's circus business, the one night stand, is largely a dream," MacNeice continued, scowling now with pampered lips. "Except for the merest and tattiest of pick-ups, drunks and flapabouts for the most part, it seldom happens. Not at least among free agents who really want to lie with each other, unless, as I say, one of them happens to be ticketed through and already travelling. And you know," he went on, "it doesn't get any easier to live with guilt. In the case of most of the neurotic rovers who transport themselves from bed to bed that I've mentioned there was a precipitating figure. One doesn't want to be that ever again."

He took his companion by the arm and lowered his voice. "As you know my dear fellow," he said, "in effect I've been twice married. And I've destroyed or dismantled about half a dozen other women's lives besides, without benefit of clerk or clergy. I have been forced to simulate nervous breakdowns myself to escape reproach or guilt. But for the exigencies of my profession, I might well have migrated to the Australian outback or wherever it is that other people go. And I have driven someone else into a lunatic asylum from which she never emerged. I mean literally. In a motor car. Through the gates. So when you get to my age you seriously consider whether to suffice yourself with ready old acquaintances, however lacking in their pristine attractions they may have become, or even with the pleasures of the inviolable imagination, rather than go through the whole human business and human guilt again. This has nothing to do with physiological aging, although everything, even the response to stripping something young and unfamiliar for the first time, changes with age. It has to do with learning from experience what the consequences of even the most casual-seeming encounters can be. And I, my dear fellow, have lain beside women in hell."

They had come to the lighted doorway of O'Turk's. MacNeice's pendant lips and cheeks composed now a mask of weary compliance. Riley went in, a broken king at nightfall.

Susan had half turned and was waiting, her fine thin shoulder against the partly opened glass door, her hair illumined from behind, the curve of her breasts and her narrowing torso in silhouette, a sheaf for the gathering.

The Baron smiled to himself. He would take it all out on her. He would gather her to-night.

woman had turned and was walking... her long hair shadual... Without ... interposed a shadow ... her suit the wind blew... behind, the sleeve of her... and her bare arm... upbore in a show for the gath...

... upbore in... little bright r... of...
... an essential corsplie... to seen.

Book 2

*B*ut it didn't turn out like that. Lying awake the next morning on the bed of pain and shame on which he had also woken the day before, the Baron, in analytic mood, and hungover as before, failed to analyse quite what, if anything specific, had gone wrong. Perhaps the demon drink, that subtle creator and destroyer of opportunity, had been the nigger in the woodpile. Perhaps, before the night was over, he had suffered a slight personality transformation; and had become silly, or sentimental, or pushful, or cantankerous, all of which were things he did, alas, occasionally become, and this had caused Susan to look upon him with an eye other than the one with which she had been taking him in before: with disfavour in fact, or askance anyway.

It had, after all, been a very long day. He had stood trial. He had unfolded his life-story in the most intimate detail to an old friend. He had attempted burglary. He had found the proofs of his ancestry to have vanished. It would have been no wonder if, in spite of being in company with a girl and having designs on her, he had suffered a small breakdown. But in any case he couldn't remember very much.

His plan had been to let it all devolve naturally from a general return to Jonathen's, where she might willingly have remained after the others had gone and he might have had his way with her. But it had failed of execution, even though he had successfully got up a little party; they had all in fact come back to where he now lay; and he was pretty sure that at a certain early stage of the proceedings he had read all the signals of acquiescence aright.

He had not of course propositioned her outright. Although in the contemporary world (with which, he was now beginning to feel, he was losing touch) people might do that, it had never been his custom. There are Rubicons and Rubicons, and in sexual matters, as in others, the Baron preferred his invisible.

Somehow or other, though, he had muffed it. He had undoubtedly got too drunk. He had spent too much time performing for the party in general and had not kept his thoughts on the pleasures in putative (or pudendive) prospect. And there was always of course the possibility that it had never been on; that such a conjunction played no part in her general outlook on their relationship, however vague or specific that might be, if indeed she had such a thing as an outlook at all, though without flattering himself the Baron did not believe in the possibility of a woman where he was concerned without.

Anyway she had in fact drifted off at some stage, taken presumably an early lift and gone. She had come over to where he was standing with Mulvaney and MacNeice, smiled at him and said: "I'm going now. Give me a ring to-morrow. Be sure now." And then she was gone.

Now that he thought of it he couldn't remember much immediately prior to her going, and nothing after it at all. Who was the lift from, if lift indeed was all it was? There had of course been too many people present. O'Turk's had been full of folk-singers of various schools and would-be self-and-otherwise-destructive proletarian playwrights; and the whole of O'Turk's, it seemed to him, had come back to Jonathen's, with or without his expressed consent. Had somebody else ... clicked with her? Some extrovert gurrier who personified her notion of ... masculinity? Had he reason to be ... jealous? Had she gone off with some bearded bullyboy to have what even the girls were now, perhaps rather oddly, calling a good fuck? At this point the Baron's whole being was pervaded by an appalling sense of being the one left out, being a mere third party, being his age (which was a sight older than she was) and being ridiculous.

Somewhat earlier the same morning, however, the object of his thoughts had been woken up by a loud knocking, a thunderous and reverberant "whack, whack, whack" on the front door of the house in Dun Laoghaire which the Baron had burgled the day before. Pulling a dressing-gown over her night-dress, her beautiful body still warm from sleep, she had made her way barefoot down the stairs, opened the front door and said a startled "hello" to a sergeant of the guards who was standing on the top step.

The Baron's waking and rising of the day before has already been exhaustively enough described. This second morning his speculations about the time element, his strainings to hear bird-song (no bird-song) milk-horses or garbage-ponies (evidently far too late for milk-horses or garbage-ponies) traffic noises (plenty of these, amounting to an almost continuous groaning and whining) in fact his attempts, such as they were, to establish what time it was, were merely on the head of an arrangement to meet Riley in the pub. However miserable he might feel in general, he did not have, he reflected, stretching his limbs with a small temporary ecstasy of relief, an appearance in a Court of Justice to contend with ... Justice. He went rigid in the bed. But he had an appointment. With the Minister for that commodity. This was the Friday. And it had once been "next Friday two weeks—after I get back from my politicking". Christ blast it. He was in no fit state now for such an encounter: long temporised over, muffed, postponed, vague of purpose, dubious of outcome, of human and social interest it was true, even of human import in terms of an old warmth of acquaintance, but fraught with dangers all the same, and in any case a terrible whirlpool to be plunged in now with his nerves agley from the ordeals of yesterday and that feeling of inferiority and failure which was his prime enemy made consanguineous with his whole being.

It was true he had once thought that his old friend might be able to throw some light on the question of his ancestry, having full access, as nobody else had, to the secret files of the day. It was also true that he had imagined he might be able to do

111

something about the seemingly inexorable processes of the law, for he must be the master, if any man was, of those particular processes. And up to a little while ago anyway the Baron had believed that he might perhaps be induced to part with some badly needed cash, for rumour at least had it that he was floating in the stuff these days.

But as for his ancestry, the Baron knew almost enough about the subject now. His research over the years, desultory and unco-ordinated though it was, had carried him just about as far as it was possible, he thought, to go; and he had only asked the Minister to make some enquiries about Richard Pigott (without revealing the reason) at a stage in the present proceedings when he had thought that any new fact he might garner would somehow be a help. He had no real stomach for any further discussion of the question of his ancestry now. It would be more important at this stage to get the Minister working on the law, but he had, quite obviously, left that too late. Even supposing he did bring the matter up now, make a clean breast of it and so forth, it was probably far too late to ask him to do anything effective to pervert the course of justice. And as for money, that had been and was, the obstacle to other converse, the thing that had prevented him from asking the Minister to do, or even to discuss, anything else. He had made a false move in relation to money; put a rather hefty brick in it as you might say; and the thought had both shamed him into avoidance and inhibited him from making use of his old acquaintance in any other way. Such things will, he reflected, happen when you're down in the mouth; and it is also a law that when you're down in the mouth you never get anything. The shabby approach went out with the Edwardians. Successful touchers nowadays were successful men.

But was he downhearted? He could not quite say why, but as soon as he was out of bed and engaged with the tannic acid his spirits began to rise. And whatever about the thought of the Minister, the thought of Susan, which, a moment ago, had been the cause of such misery, now began to attain something like the penumbra of promise it should have. Somehow, while the thought of her created a void, she filled it too; and if the night before he had been merely impatient to have access to her physical person, and to enjoy some power of disposition over her parts and members without much reference to the personality involved, this morning it was her individual presence and responses, the radiance of her total being that he wanted, to inform his day and cause, as, it seemed to him now, only it could, the exclusion of all else, including his ancestry and the troubles it had created for him.

She had said to ring her. Well, he would. But meantime he was quite cheered up. It seemed to him now, afoot and astir, that there were elements of hope in all the things that he and she were connected in together. He decided to take some reading matter with him to Jonathen's dark lavatory. He could even risk another dip into T. D. Sullivan's *Recollections of Troubled Times In Irish Politics*.

"As for Mr P. J. Meehan, he was no traitor, but a patriotic and honorable gentleman. In the summer of 1865 he had come to Ireland from New York, on business connected with the organisation, bringing some documents. These he had the misfortune to lose at the Kingstown railway station, near Dublin (July 22nd, 1865). They were found by a telegraph messenger, who took them to the postmistress, by whom they were handed over to the Superintendent of the Kingstown police, who, in his turn, delivered them to the authorities at Dublin Castle. The loss of the papers was a pure accident, but it was an unpleasant incident of the Brotherhood. They stormed against Mr Meehan. If they confined themselves to blaming him for not having been more careful of the papers entrusted to him they would have had right and reason on their side, but they went far beyond that point, and accusations of treachery and treason were freely sped about. In times of excitement charges of that kind find ready credence, gather bulk and weight as they go along, and sink into the public mind. Mr Meehan was adjudged a traitor by some council or committee of the Brotherhood, and held to have incurred the penalty of death. Pending the threatened execution they gave him the sinister nickname of "The Man of the Documents".

*The appellation did not come well from men who at that very time were carelessly keeping in their possession hundreds of compromising documents, the seizure of which, by the police, a few weeks afterwards, put all the threads of the conspiracy into the hands of the Government, and enabled them to raid the organisation as a fox might ravage a poultry yard. They talked of "The Man of the Documents"—the real "Men of the Documents" were the editors and managers of **The Irish People**. Detective Hughes, one of the police party who cleared out the office, deposed before the Special Commission that he and they brought away from that emporium more than 1,000 letters!*

Five years after his return to America, Mr Meehan was dangerously wounded by a pistol-shot in New York, but the affair had no relation to the trouble about the "documents"."

After a while Susan began to find the hallway, clad as she was, uncomfortably cold; and so she invited the sergeant and the young policeman who accompanied him downstairs for a cup of tea. In spite of the news they had brought she was at least part conscious of the effect that her sleep tousled appearance and garb was having on them; and as she proferred the invitation and then turned and preceded them down the stairs her whole demeanour was ever so slightly affected by the fact that she was a girl in a night-dress who had just been woken out of her bed, and they, although policemen, were two nice-looking and comparatively bright fellows just in off the morning street. She felt, in short, slightly vulnerable and unprotected and she knew they found her so as well, in some part of their unofficial being. This gave her some pleasure, in spite of the news they had brought.

"Now, let's get this straight," said Riley, as soon as they were settled with the drinks. "There was a box. Way back at least, there was a box."

The Baron nodded assent.

"Then there was no box."

"They said there was no box."

"Right. But subsequent to that, when Susan came along, then there was a box once more."

"Er, yes. According to Susan, yes. There was a box in that shed."

"But after that again, when you went out there yesterday, there was no box."

"That's right."

"No box at all, in the shed, in the house or otherwise."

"No box at all, upstairs, downstairs or in my lady's chamber," said the Baron. He had been in her chamber too, but he said nothing about his sensations while there.

"And you have only her word for it that there ever was a box in that shed."

"Well, yes. I suppose so. Yes."

"And then last night, when you've already been out there and smashed in the door, she tells you it's gone."

"Yes."

"Which you already know."

"Yes."

"She spotted the door rather quickly."

"She was back there after work."

There was a pause. "Well look, Dickon," Riley said. "I have a thing here that may interest you. As a matter of fact I had it last night. I got it in the post when I went home, but I didn't like to tell you about it last night because your mind appeared to be on other things. In the earlier part of the proceedings anyway."

"I'd be glad to know what it is, when you have the time, and if it isn't too much trouble," replied the Baron sarcastically.

For answer Riley pulled some papers out of his pocket. They were mimeographed sheets, clipped together and headed "G. Granville Barker, Book and Manuscript Dealer, 44

Portugal Chambers, London, E.C. 4. Recent Acquisitions of Importance."

One item on the first sheet was marked in red, presumably by Riley, for he now jabbed at it with an insistent forefinger.

"Historically important memorabilia of Richard Pigott the Forger, letters from Charles Stewart Parnell and related material," the Baron read. "A highly important cache which includes unpublished and hitherto unknown letters to Pigott from C. S. Parnell and Edward Caulfield Houston as well as many items of prime importance in Pigott and Parnell biography, indispensable to future researchers. Full description of material, Photo-stats of selected items on application."

The Baron sat in silence for a few moments.

"Where did you get this?" he asked then.

"This fellow is a book and manuscript dealer," Riley answered. "And I've had some dealings with him over manuscripts. Now normally speaking these sharks don't like us mere providers of the raw material to know what they've got and what they're selling. There's often a bit of hugger mugger, you know—people selling letters from their friends about money and mistresses, and maybe even selling what they don't own."

"Mayhap a bit of forgery," said the Baron, smiling somewhat grimly in spite of himself.

"Mayhap," said Riley. "But anyway, this fellow and I are old pals. We were at school together as a matter of fact, and he sends me these circulars because it amuses me to know what some of my confreres are flogging. The condition is I keep my mouth shut."

"You're good at that," conceded the Baron.

"You bet your sweet bippy I am," said Riley. "But in any case the fact is that I've been on the blower to him this morning and so I've got some more to tell you, but let me preface it by saying that no dealer will ever disclose his sources of supply because as I've said there are often underhand aspects to his dealings. In fact, you might say, the majority of manuscript

116

dealers are fences, no more and no less. Howsomever, after a little Chinese diplomacy I did ask this fellow straight out where he'd got the stuff. All he would say was "an Irish source". Then I told him I was interested because I knew somebody who believed himself to be a relative of Pigott's. That was true enough. I told him also that my man had some material but was more likely to be a purchaser than a vendor. That wasn't so true and I don't know whether he believed me or not. I asked him for a description of the stuff and, well, he said there were letters from Parnell about a business transaction, there were miscellaneous other letters and household documents as he called them—I elicited that he meant bills and receipts—and there were dirty pictures. We had quite a laugh about that."

"Did he say anything about Joyce letters?" asked the Baron.

"He did not," said Riley. "Maybe for some reason best known to his nefarious self he's selling them separately. I couldn't list the contents of *your* box and ask him had he got this or got that because he would have smelled a rat. I did ask him if he would send me a list of what he'd got and he said that if my man would write to him in confidence he would consider whether it would be possible to send him an itemised list. I said that my man would naturally be interested in other relatives and he said of course he couldn't disclose the source without permission. Looking back on the conversation I am not even sure that he has actually got the stuff. He may have only seen it. The phrase he kept using was 'the material on offer contains'."

He looked at his friend. "I'm sorry," he said. "That's as far as I got. Remember I was in a coin box with the pips going all the time, and that although we're supposed to be pals, this fellow is a bollocks and the telephone is not my medium."

"It's the same stuff," the Baron said.

"It looks like it," said Riley.

"The contents of that box have been flogged ... or put on offer."

"Again it looks like it."

"By an Irish source."

"That's what the man said."

"Susan."

"Surely not. Surely it's much more likely to be them."

"They wouldn't have sold the dirty pictures. Or put them on offer. Not in a million years. No, it was ... her. She had a look inside that box for some reason. Maybe something I said. It would be natural enough for her to have a look anyway. She must have put two and two together and seen she was on to a good thing. She's cleverer than I thought."

"There is one snag, though," Riley said.

"What's that?"

"Is she literate and intelligent enough to know about Parnell and Pigott and to figure out what the stuff was? How literate is she?"

"She's literate enough for somebody to cod himself about her if he was ... fond of her," said the Baron drily. "And as far as Parnell and Pigott are concerned, I'm afraid I brought them into the conversation."

"You what?"

"I brought them into the conversation, I'm afraid. I suppose I wanted to unburden myself to her in some way or other, make her a party to things in some way. I sort of told her the story. There was Cronin's television programme about Parnell. You know how it is. I wanted to talk. Oh, I didn't tell her about myself and my connection with anything. I just rambled on in a sort of witty, discursive and learned way about Parnell. And Pigott. I was being professorial."

"I can hear you at it. You were making deception more deceitful. Bringing her into things indeed. Professorial indeed. You must be very fond of her and she must have had quite a lot to think about if your discourse was fresh in her mind when she opened the box. If she opened the box."

"God knows what else she has figured out by now."

"God knows. You may not be the only one playing a double game. Has she the nerve for that? I mean is she cool enough? She would want to be rather cruel as well, wouldn't she? I mean to open the box, realise it was the stuff inside you were after and that it must be valuable; and then begin the process of flogging it while still looking you in the eye and leading you on, smiling as she eyed you? Especially when there was no need. She could just have flogged the stuff and kissed you good-bye.

118

Or not kissed you good-bye—whichever she preferred."

A silence had fallen as Susan and her two companions sipped the last of the tea she had made. The sergeant had given her all the relevant information he possessed and also such advice as seemed to him suitable in the circumstances. In doing so he had been eagerly and deferentially supported by his young companion. There had followed a brief interval of general conversation to which all three had contributed as best they might. This was now at an end; and perhaps because nobody seemed able to find anything more to say, Susan's feelings about being in a state of partial undress while her two companions were, to say the least, fully clad, began to change. Instead of a mild feeling of pleasure at being an object of obvious attraction she began to experience a sense of disadvantage. She was getting particularly fed up of the comparatively undisguised regard of the junior of the two and besides she very much wanted now to think her own thoughts. It was with relief and pleasure therefore that she saw the sergeant at last reaching for his cap.

She would. She would certainly come round to the station later in the day and she was really very grateful for the trouble they had gone to. Of course naturally she had not quite taken in the news yet. Even though you might not be that close to somebody it was always a terrible shock. Were they sure they wouldn't like another cup of tea?

"But how the hell would she know anything about fellows who deal in papers, manuscripts, that kind of stuff?"

"Oh, there's no difficulty about that. He advertises in "Hibernia". 'Rare books and manuscripts wanted, mss, historical material, etc. Top prices negotiated'. Besides, old son, she may have a boy-friend who ... has wised her up."

"To believe that she was acting under advisal like that would be to attribute a really extreme degree of duplicity to her," remarked the Baron tonelessly.

"Put her almost in the Mata Hari class," agreed Riley. "But

119

d'ye know in a way I favour the tremulous old pair of religious maniacs. Supposing they really knew nothing about your father's ancestry but your sudden re-appearance and your blather about the box causes them to hunt it up and open it. Supposing they examine the contents in the light of what you have been telling them. Supposing they decide the stuff is valuable. Supposing they need money? Supposing they read "Hibernia"? Do they need money? Do they read "Hibernia"?"

"I really don't know. He was some sort of a Customs man. I presume he'd have a pension and I imagine they'd own that house."

"The alternative supposition is that they knew about Pigott all along but for some reason wanted to conceal that knowledge from you. Your sudden re-appearance and your questionings about the box causes them to decide to get rid of the contents, but their cupidity or their need will not allow them simply to throw it all out. They throw out the box all right—that's how Susan finds it in the shed—but they put the stuff in the hands of our dealer friend. What better way to get rid of it after all? Have it wheeled off somewhere, and kept, like you say, under bomb-proof glass, at an even temperature and pressure?"

"It isn't a very good way of concealing the connection."

"It's a splendid way of concealing the connection, supposing that was what they were worried about. The neighbours don't know because the dealer keeps his mouth shut about the source. You don't know either because there are often conditions attached to those transactions which the purchaser has to observe. It may have been you they were worried about. It may even be that they thought they had a duty to keep you in ignorance. It may also be that they thought you were telling the world and his wife about your ancestry and that sooner or later you would disgrace them too, however remote their connection. This way they bind everybody to secrecy and that's the end of the matter."

"But posterity?"

"You must be joking. In Ireland nobody gives a bugger about posterity. At least not among their sort of people. Posterity is a chimera that burdens only certain classes.

Aristocrats perhaps. Revolutionaries, certainly. But artists in especial."

"I still do not believe they would have sold the pictures of naked girls hanging by the wrists from the ceiling, or strapped to wheels, or spreadeagled face down on tables."

"H'mm. I'm not so sure. If those pictures were connected with an abstraction called history and if consequently their connection with real life was obscured they might."

"If it was her it's ... a bit of a shock."

"Whereas if it was them ... . That would certainly be better. But I can't judge because I don't know enough about them. Tell me something more about your uncle. What was he interested in? What were his hobbies?"

"He was interested in being respectable," replied the Baron. "And that was his hobby. Being respectable."

After thinking things over Susan had decided to have a good look round the house, to search it in fact, and to read whatever papers and documents relevant to the situation it might contain.

In the heavily furnished room with many ikons and representations of suffering—Christ crowned with thorns and the Madonna with her heart seven times pierced by some drunken knife-thrower among them—there was an old-fashioned bureau with little drawers on each side and a ledge that you pulled down to write on. She decided to start with this and in the very first drawer she opened she found, amongst other things, a carefully scissored out newspaper photograph which showed Mr Ronald Ponsonby, the artist, and Mr J. J. Fogarty, the Minister for Justice, chatting together over a glass of some wine-like liquid. The caption said the photograph had been taken at the opening of an exhibition of the former's paintings by the latter at the Hibernian Gallery. Somewhat puzzled, she continued her search.

At the bottom of this drawer there were also two framed photographs laid flat. She surmised they had been removed at some stage from the collection of framed wedding and other photographs on the mantlepiece. One was possibly a first-communion photograph of a curly haired boy in white suit; and the other was a snapshot of uncertain provenance which showed a smiling stripling in white flannels and a blazer holding a tennis racket aslant.

Kneeling on the floor by the bureau Susan compared all three photographs together; and as she examined and compared them she said first, "Golly"; and then, in a louder tone: "Christ". It was plain that she had a good deal more thinking to do.

"I only want something that will give me a clue," said Riley. "Can you manage an epiphany of any sort?"

"Well, " said the Baron after a pause, "the big, revelation-through-action, existential crisis of his life was probably the controversy about women wearing shorts in the Badminton Club."

"That sounds very promising," said Riley. "Proceed."

"He was," began the Baron after a moment of reflection, "secretary of the Badminton Club at home in Ballywhidder; and for a politician, which in some sort he must have been to achieve that post, and a man of caution, which he most certainly was by nature, he seems to have behaved with what almost amounted to recklessness during the affair. Perhaps, like many politicians, at the fateful moment he overestimated his influence, his consequence, or his powers of blackmail. Anyway he threatened to resign from the committee on the issue of whether women members should be allowed to wear shorts or not and he was taken up on it. Considering the subject of the row I am tempted to make a bad pun and say that he went out on a limb."

"Oh make it, make it by all means," said Riley.

But the Baron continued impassively.

"The badminton took place in a hall which was occasionally used for other purposes, probably dances, concerts and whist drives. The club had been formed largely through my uncle's recruitment of fellow enthusiasts, all of them presumably new to the game. When the row developed it had been in existence for, I suppose, about ten years and it was highly important to him in several ways: it was a place to go on winter evenings where he could be sure of a welcome; it provided satisfactions for his ambitions and his organising powers; and the game itself was a form of enjoyable physical recreation which he probably needed, for he was, in his own way, something of an athlete. In fact the game of badminton and the administrative duties it involved him in constituted a large part of his social, and probably his imaginative, life.

"Of course I only became aware that a row was in progress through the sort of hugger mugger that is made to surround adult deliberations when you are a child. I suppose I must have been about twelve at the time. Apart from the fact that words like indecent, outrageous, immodest, shameless et cetera were used in front of me during the prolonged if sotto voce discussions of the matter that took place at meal-times and in their bedroom at night with the door open—the low give and take of those voices will be with me when I die—I think I did know somehow that there was something wrong with women wearing shorts. We are indoctrinated early in mysterious ways. But I would not have known because my own erotic impulses were in any way involved, though that in my youth was a sure test of evil. No, quite definitely: I had an early and passionate puberty to be sure, for I must still have been at the convent school—which means I was under six—when I had that long delightful imagining about all the girls being made to lie on the frozen lake in their knickers, the first time I ever remember a true erection and the true sweetness, but I cannot remember taking any sort of prurient interest in the question of the bad girls in their shorts at the Badminton Club, as revealed to me through the various conferences, whisperings and pacings up and down. They belonged, it seems, to the adult world, governed by different erotic stimuli and obeying different laws.

Nor do I know how many females were involved, what age they were, whether it was a question of the generation gap or whether some matrons even were among the number. However, a conversation that I particularly remember took place one evening at tea. There had been a lot of oblique chat about the crisis, supposedly engaged in on the assumption that I would not know what it was about. At length my uncle pushed away his plate of grease and egg-yolk and said bitterly, 'I knew it was a mistake to have a mixed club to begin with.'

" 'It was indeed,' concurred my aunt, taking a deliberate sip from her cup.

'That was my doing,' said my uncle.

'Ah no Joe,' said my aunt. 'Don't blame yourself for that. How were you to know the sort of thing would creep in. And weren't they very instrumental in the beginning in getting the club going?'

'How was I to know?' asked my uncle. 'The simple answer to that is I should have known. That's the simple answer.'

'Ah sure you couldn't,' argued my aunt.

'I would have guessed it wouldn't be good for faith or morals in the long run anyway,' said my Uncle. 'It's my own fault,' he added after a pause. 'And bitterly I've lived to regret it.'

"There was silence for a while. 'Yes indeed,' said my aunt then. 'They haven't much modesty, I suppose, Protestant girls. But don't blame yourself too much, for as it turns out aren't our own as bad.'

"This was, as I say, one of the few conversations that gave me any sort of concrete clues as to numbers, alignments and sympathies. From other conversations I do seem to remember "the younger set" being a term of opprobium, and I have the definite impression that my uncle started out with the support of the older members of the committee; that he acted in the beginning on the assumption that he would of course receive backing all round; that he was disappointed in the younger males and that finally even the older members fell away from his side, adopting, or pretending to adopt, progressive views, and perhaps finding the new exposures in the club so delightful that they pretended to casual now-what's-all-the-fuss-about progressive views to ensure themselves little visual pangs. One way or another support fell away very rapidly and from being debated in an initial atmosphere of agreement in committee the matter went to a general meeting at which my uncle's motion about modesty in dress was soundly defeated, indeed if I may make another pun of sorts, laughed out of court."

Riley spluttered into his glass. "By God that's even better," he averred.

"That was what broke him in the end," continued the Baron, "and broke his spirit too, the ridicule. I remember knowing something about the general meeting, and I overheard the conversation in the bedroom that night during which he said over and over again, 'some of them were laughing' and spoke of 'silly billies at the back who had nothing better to do than to make a joke out of the whole thing.'

"What part did she play in it all? Did she ... egg him on? Towards his political doom? Again I cannot be certain, but my impression is that she very definitely did. It surprises me that they could discuss the matter together at all, even in the kind of words that they used. I mean surely such discussions ought to have created some embarrassment or even heat between them, particularly when conducted in hushed monotones in the bedroom at night, as I remember they frequently were. Perhaps they did. The shorts of the day I seem to recollect—whether I saw any of the controversial wearers or not—as being flannel, not linen or cotton, what was inaccurately called white flannel, for it was in fact off-white or cream coloured. They came to about four inches above the knee. But where would I have seen them? Am I super-imposing photographs I have seen since of Suzanne Lenglen or Helen Wills Moody or somebody on memory?

"Not very revealing anyway, you will say; yet my retrospective memory or mere retrospective imagination suggests—which, as I have said, would not have occurred to me then—that they were becoming enough about the rump. In fact one of the things that intrigues me now is this: was it the legs or arses? I mean which were the greatest danger to his otherwise dormant libido and therefore to be conceived of as a likely danger to the libidos of others? Which, if either, was the preponderant danger, limb or haunch? The danger of the leg was more or less traditional and must have occurred to him before; indeed, the erotic powers of that member would have been bruited abroad by then in the talkies at least, even if not yet in the lower class of English Sunday newspaper. But if he discovered the arses were intriguing him it must have been a shock, for I do not think arses were admitted into the Irish imagination in the late nineteen twenties and hence I am sure

125

were seldom fondled or squeezed either, for surely the imaginative disturbance has to come first? If this was the first time the joys of behinds had occurred to him, visual or actual, I am sure he felt very depraved. And if that was the case he must have felt acutely the imminent possibility of others being depraved also.

"This would explain his ire, his anxiety and his recklessness in making a do or die issue of the matter. I mean much more than if it was merely the legs, whose powers of erotic attraction were admitted, even beginning to be publicised, which were bothering him. For it is surely the unadmitted, forcing itself suddenly in, that really sets the puritan off on his courageous moral crusades? All in all I think it must have been those cream flannel behinds which really aggravated him.

"Or was it, God help us, merely dull abstract theory, a rule of thumb extension of commandments and sermons which set him off? One way or another it was a bad day for him when he raised the matter in committee. The ridicule he endured at the general meeting he apparently felt continued on his ordinary visits to the club after he had resigned the secretaryship. He felt he was being jeered at even while he was playing. He spoke of sniggerings, corner boys laughing at him behind their hands. Whether this was imagination or not he shortly afterwards resigned his ordinary membership also and never went again to the club he had founded. After that he had no place to go on the winter evenings where he could be sure of a welcome and be a much-greeted and important man. In view of that sacrifice I can't really see him selling the dirty pictures now."

"But you never know, do you?" said Riley after a pause. "Too long a sacrifice can make a stone of the heart."

In O'Turk's they were also, by a curious coincidence, and early in the morning though it was, discussing the subject of women's apparel.

"They'll soon be wearin' nothin' at all," said one customer, folding his Daily Mirror and evidently referring to something therein.

"An unfortunate, paganised country, England," said the

barman, apparently in response.

"But sure aren't they walkin' up and down Grafton Street in their milli-skirts or whatever they're called," asked a second customer. "Talk about a leg show in the Theatre Royal. Sure Grafton Street is twice as bad."

"They have to get a fella," said the barman. "It's as simple as that. Open and shut. No fella will buy a pig in a poke these days. They have to show their wares to the public whether they like it or not."

"You know I don't really think that many women understand the male response to visual stimulation," said a well-dressed individual further down the bar who might have been an actor or a mountebank of some sort. "I remember when I was in a touring show in England a few years ago. I'm afraid it wasn't much of a show, but the girls were what you might call rather scantily clad. They were just young hopefuls like you'd find in any such touring show, not strippers or anything like that, and in those days anyway the girls didn't know the half of it. Well at the afternoon shows anyway we used to get mostly male audiences and you know they weren't very responsive with the applause. This used to bother the girls quite a bit and one day one of them asked me about it. 'Why don't they ever applaud the big number?' she said. 'They just seem to sit there in silence all the time.' 'Well,' I said, 'with this kind of show silence is applause, if you know what I mean,' but she didn't."

"You want to go to Birmingham," said another customer. "That's where you'd see things. When I was there I used to go to a joint called the Jungle Club and honest to God you wouldn't believe it. Talk about takin' it all off. Begod ye'd see more in the Jungle Club that ye'd bargain for. Lovely young mottes strippin' off in front of you too there were, not just ould stagers."

"An unfortunate God-forsaken country," said the barman. "And booked for a fall."

"Did ye ever see a lassie in a lion's cage?" demanded a near-by pint-drinker. "I seen that in Leeds. Tied up without a stitch on her, she was, an' the lions jumpin' round and growlin'."

"There was more than the lions jumpin' round and growlin'

I'd lay," said the first customer, amid general laughter.

The one who had been addressed as Doctor on the previous day now spoke up from the table where he sat behind the *Sporting Chronicle* and a large dock glass of pale, dry sherry. "Rich women will do anything to get into show biz," he declared. "Anything. There's a terrible element of exhibitionism in them all."

This was followed by a short, mystified silence.

Then: "There were two auld bachelor fellows lived up our way in Stoneybatter," said a hitherto silent individual in black who sat on his own at the end of the counter. "Called themselves Smith, but they were really sons of Pigott the forger—everybody knew that. One of them was a real dandy. He used to wear a bowler hat and a carnation in his buttonhole night, noon and morning. The other one was a quare sort of a hawk and when the dandy fellow died he was left there on his own. You'd see him comin' down the street snufflin' and mutterin' to himself and gawkin' at the mottes.

"Well there were two or three wild young brassers in the buildings there in those days that went on the game afterwards and this auld fellow used to have a couple of them in and he'd give them a few bob to take off their clothes for him. That's all he ever wanted them to do, just strip off the togs and stand there. And they'd do it for him. Wild young wans, ye know. He'd give them maybe four or five bob for standin' there in their skin for half an hour gigglin' at him an' him lookin' at them. This was thirty years ago and four or five bob was big money in those days. Just stand there and let on ye hate it, he'd say to them. Let on yer miserable. Well, it was found out of course. The brassers told somebody and he hanged himself. His windas were broken and the people were goin' to lynch him and have the law on him and all sorts of things and the upshot was he hanged himself in the front parlour. The house was only knocked down a few years ago. Ponsonby's the coal people had it after. Of course they called themselves Smith. But it was well known in the locality who they were."

"Well, well, well. The fall of the house of Pigott," said a member of the audience after a suitable silence.

"Aye, aye, aye. The last of the line," said another

sententiously.

"Where ignorance is bliss 'tis folly to be wise," said the one commonly addressed as doctor from behind the *Sporting Chronicle,* but the remark was again allowed to pass in silence.

"That fellow we were talkin' about yesterday, didn't somebody say his name was Pigott?" asked somebody else after a brief interval.

"Oh he has nothin' to do with Pigott the forger," said the first customer dogmatically. "Nothin' whatever. He was got sub rosa by some Duke or Colonel. Sure didn't his Excellency here say yesterday he only took the name Pigott by deed poll?"

"Oh, dark, dark, dark amid the blaze of noon," said the one referred to.

"What happened to him yesterday, I wonder," asked the barman to change the subject, the question being more or less addressed to the invisible authority.

"Remanded at his majesty's pleasure," said the one more or less addressed without lowering his newspaper.

"Is that so?" asked the barman.

The rest remained silent. No-one was willing to disclose his ignorance of whatever might be meant by that.

Susan's motives for searching through drawers and reading such papers as she might find there had now been intensified, to say the least. In the same bureau, though not in the same drawer, she had found some other papers which appeared to name the Baron and even one which referred to herself. It took her a little while to grasp their full significance, but then she realised that what was therein could change her whole life, to put it mildly, and so she searched everywhere that occurred to her for more, finding a bank statement which was significant and dozens of old receipts and receipted bills, which weren't.

But the attic at the top of a house is often, in Ireland, the repository where the bulk of the available information about the past and about family relationships is stored. Though not yet out of her nightdress, therefore, she had now arrived at the attic and was about to begin a survey of whatever it might contain. She was still thinking furiously.

129

The Baron also had some thinking to do. Riley, full of resource, had gone off to elicit the aid of a local book and manuscript dealer he knew who might be induced to pretend to an interest in the Pigott material and phone the fellow in London. That way, it had been agreed between them, a little more might be found out about where the London stuff had come from, or a deal of some sort might even be made by means of which it could perhaps be got back to Dublin in time for production in Court on Monday morning, as the Baron's property or otherwise.

"You never know your luck," Riley said. "It's an ill sort of a wind that doesn't blow some bloody good while it's at it. This bod here in Dublin is a genuinely decent fellow. So much so that his humanity, or at least his regard for myself, may even take precedence over his occupation. And we may as well try to take advantage of the fact that this stuff is now on offer in a free market economy. Supposing my Dublin dealer decides that it is worth a great deal more with a story and a substantiation behind it? Well, you're the story and you're the substantiation, so he might be induced to gamble; and he's in a position to buy it on the telephone and have it flown back to Dublin on an Aer Fungus jet if he wants to. I might even make an offer myself. Never say die. There could still be dirty pictures being passed round for inspection in the Court on Monday morning. And at the very least we might find out, if I may put it that way, who flogged the bloody stuff."

Which, to the Baron, though he would not have confessed that, even to Riley, was now the important thing. He must know who had done this, and know specifically whether Susan had. He began to think of her examining the stuff, sitting on the floor in the attic in this other house perhaps, as he had once done in the house in Ballywhidder, and being moved to rising excitement by the glimpse of gain as he had once been by the glimpse of ancestral identity. He formed a disturbing mental image of her examining the photographs, her head bent, her hair like a dark curtain over her face; and then he switched to a dismaying one of her consulting a boy-friend about what she had discovered. He wanted to go on thinking about her and her possible motives, and yet the subject didn't bear thinking of;

130

and so it was that he was pleased in a way to be joined by an acquaintance who had now entered the pub.

This was a lecturer in the Celtic Institute who had attained a large local reputation as a writer of essays and short reviews in uninfluential journals. The fact of the Baron's presence in the place appeared to have created a certain commotion in his spirit and the severe note of his "Ah, M'sieu le Baron" suggested a mind burdened with concern. He had the grace though immediately to offer the Baron a drink.

"M'sieu le Baron will have ahh one of your larger gins and tonics," he said after he had succeeded in procuring the barman's attention with much angular gesturing and spillings of ash from a Player's cigarette.

"Gins and Roses," corrected the Baron, inwardly pleased and without petulance.

"And he will have ahh also some advice," the other added.

"Not for Jasus sake at this hour of the morning," said the Baron as softly as he could. "Nor for the sake of his blessed mother in the hearing of the barman either, for I owe him a little money and those in need of advice are per se untrustworthy."

"Oh yes, he will have also some advice," said the other sternly. "Advice which has nothing to do with whatever sums he owes or does not owe this one or that one, although if I may say so the coffee houses and other places of resort are in fact buzzing with strange rumours which apparently have to do with monetary transactions."

So it was out then, thought the Baron, sensing in the city around him immense sardonicisms, malices, gratifications, curiosities.

"I never engage in monetary transactions these days," he said lightly, nervously, swallowing a large portion of the large gin which had come.

"Look here," said the other. "I am a member of that body which Goldsmith called the strolling tribe of mortals and I spend a good deal more time than most in centres of assembly, gossip and report, so I know what I'm talking about. However, since there does seem to be even more vagueness than usual in the whispers in this instance I have ascertained nothing beyond the fact that you are in some sort of financial trouble or some sort of financial disgrace, which is not, if I may say so, an unusual state for you to be in. But since that is not the matter about which I intended to give you counsel we will not concern ourselves any further with it."

The Baron's relief was great. Anything but that.

The other leaned forward earnestly. "The matter about which I wish to speak," he said, "is of a more important and more delicate nature than any mere transaction you may have got yourself mixed up in." He pointed accusingly, cigarette gripped in a triangulation of lean, ash-stained fingers. "It is said in the high ways and by ways," he declared, "that you are about to get married again."

The Baron made a gesture which began in surprise and then dissipated itself in mid air into helpless unwillingness to make any comment at all; but the other continued to lean obliviously towards him, his jaws working on what was to come.

"And if I know you, as I believe I have the honour to do," he said, "the likelihood is that romantic attraction rather than circumstantial advantage or plain, down ·to earth sexual convenience will be the basis of your intent."

"It is absolute rubbish," began the Baron, robbed of other retort by such a preposterous charge; and fiercely annoyed at the same time that he should be the subject of this kind of speculation. But he might as well have said nothing.

"For the truth of the matter is," his acquaintance continued, "that you and I have romantic sensibilities. We had an early vision and a boundless hope. We knew the wild upsurge of the heart that comes with the first held glance from under dark eyelashes, with the look sustained longer than ordinary converse would warrant, with the apparently accidental touching of hands. Having known this once, we will always desire it again. And it may even be that we will blind ourselves recurrently to the consequences."

He brushed away a tear. "But you know as well as I do," he said sternly, "that the romantic is in the ridiculous situation of the man who tries to have his cake and eat it at the same time. It must surely be clear to you by now that it is impossible for the extraordinary promise of another's being to survive the rapacities that make up most sexual converse; that the inchoate yearnings and the actual satisfactions given us to enjoy are at odds, self-cancelling, mutually destructive; and that the more intense the latter are, the less likelihood is there that the beautiful illusion can survive them."

There was a brief, sad silence between them. The Baron said nothing, but the other did not care. Being a university lecturer he was accustomed to silent audiences, to solitary canterings over the downs and uplands of his own thought.

"And not only is sexual possession destructive of the romantic hope and glimpse of possibility, whatever it was," he continued, "but the opposite is the case as well. Any sort of elevation of the other party into an ideal being or even a precious object diminishes sexual pleasure to a point where it is paltry and insignificant compared to the real thing. Those who achieve the true excitation care for the other party only as a vessel or vehicle of pleasure."

There was another short pause. "But what," asked the Baron humbly, "about Blake's lineaments of gratified desire?"

"I should have thought," replied the other, "that you would know the answer to that. The divine Marquis himself bids us to explore the seraglios of Africa, Asia and southern Europe, and to ask among the masters of sensuality we find there which of them is concerned about giving pleasure to the helpless individuals they choose as partners. They make demands, he says, and they are satisfied; they give orders and the other party is forbidden to murmur."

"Bedad," said the Baron.

"Among them, he says, are those proud spirits who immediately punish the impertinence of the other party if he or she achieves simultaneous gratification. What is it, he asks, that one desires when taking one's pleasures? Simply that everything around us be occupied with nothing but us, think of nothing but us, care for us only. If the object we employ demands pleasure too, it is less concerned with us than it is with itself, and our ecstasy is consequently diluted. He goes on to say, my dear Baron, that every man wishes to be a despot in this at least, and that witnessing at the exquisite moment another enjoy as he enjoys impairs the wonderful pleasure of despotism. He adds further—but this we can discount, perhaps, for we all, do we not, know his proclivities?—that it is preferable to have the object experience pain."

"A proper caution, the same Marquis," murmured the Baron.

The newspapers had been of little interest to her and she now threw aside the last of the pornographic books with some anger. She was not an especially prudish, or an especially romantic girl; but she found them deeply antipathetic. They were, she reflected, cold. As cold as the grave.

At this stage the door of the pub opened and Riley came gravely in. The lecturer swivelled round and intruded the bell on the wall behind him with a long, nicotine-stained middle finger.

"Bring these genlemen whatever they desire," he said to the ever-alert apprentice who appeared. "I myself will have a large Scotch and water."

He turned to Riley. "I need it," he said. "The Baron and I have been discussing the dangers of disillusionments of romantic attraction, always a very painful subject for me. We have been talking of the attempt to, so to speak, garner the ungarnerable, the disappointment that is inevitably in store for him who trembles before beauty as before a chalice of the mysteries once he has made that same beauty the companion of his pleasures. I need hardly tell you, my dear Patrick, that in the idea of ecstasy propounded by the great Provencal poets there was no question of sexual commerce of any kind with the eh ... piece who was supposed to be the object of the poet's love."

"Maybe not,", said Riley. "But what about a little bit of fun and friendship instead of the romantic fulfillment jag? I mean now that we're all getting older?"

The lecturer gulped his whiskey and squared his shoulders, as if gathering the strength to resist an attack on another front.

"True sexual pleasure," he said, "is not only incompatible

with romantic illusion, but is incompatible even with any sort of mutual liking and regard."

"Oh come now," said the Baron. "Lots of people hump each other and get on quite well in between."

The lecturer laughed bronchially, spilling great quantities of ash in the process. "Apart from the fact that they may be business partners, parents of the same children or co-tenants of the same house or the like of that, of course it is obviously possible for two people to remain friends, even to enjoy a tolerant and happy old age together, become, as you might say, Darby and Joan, while engaging, or subsequent to engaging in certain forms of sexual commerce with each other; indeed many people seem to feel that it's the same case as going to a football match, that it's better to have the company of somebody you like during the performance rather than the company of somebody you don't like or don't know. But, my dear chap, you know as well as I do that in order to retain this kind of amicability they are forced to deny themselves certain primary ecstasies."

He glanced over his shoulder, and, having satisfied himself that everybody was listening, lowered his voice dramatically so that it echoed round the pub. "The fact is," he said, "that in most educated tastes there is some element of preference for victimage, however playful."

"Ah yes," said Riley. "That often tears it."

"But you might strike it lucky," said the Baron. Abby? Susan?

"The odds are against it," replied the lecturer severely. "In the case of this sort of preference as in that of many others, the odds are against the possibility of conjunction, except perhaps a delusory conjunction based on the British principle of compromise and contentment with half measures."

He produced the red spotted handkerchief and blew his nose. "Let me tell you my own sad story," he said, intruding the bell again.

Riley and the Baron murmured their willingness to listen.

"When I was nine years and three months of age I was confirmed into the One, Holy, Roman, Catholic and Apostolic Church by His Excellency the Bishop of Elphin. As a reward for having achieved my new status as a full member of the communion of saints my parents took me to see a circus which had pitched its tent on the fair green of the county town of Roscommon. It was the fifteenth of August, a beautiful warm summer night. A harvest moon was shining and the scent of new mown hay was everywhere. In the tent itself there was a rich smell of ripe, crushed grass. We sat, as was proper for the occasion, in the most expensive seats, a sort of raised embankment directly abutting on the arena. After the entertainment had been under way for some time a girl entered with her partner. She had long limbs, dark hair and, even at that stage, a sulky look, as if contemptuous of the people present and reluctant to perform for them. From the tenor of the announcement made by the ring-master it appeared that she was about to do, or perhaps only to endure, something especially unpleasant, difficult and even dangerous, but what the nature of the exhibition she was about to give was I do not know, for whatever it was it went wrong.

"To begin with she lay down on some canvas on the floor of the arena and raised her legs. A rope with two rings on the end of it was then lowered from above and into these, assisted and supervised by her male companion, she proceeded to insert her feet and ankles. The rope apparently devolved from some sort of pulley arrangement up in the comparative gloom and when she had secured a grip with foot and ankle her companion crossed the ring to where the other end was secured and proceeded to haul her upwards. I still remember the slight scraping noise her shoulders and head made as they left the canvas.

"He hauled her up in the usual fashion of a man hauling in a rope, hand over hand, so that she rose rather jerkily, her lips slightly parted as if in anxiety, her eyes fixed on some point at the back of the tent, her hands on her hips and her dark hair hanging down. Then something happened. The man hauled at the rope. The girl swayed and jerked slightly but her upward progress was impeded. The rope was evidently stuck in the pulley.

"When it became evident that something was wrong she began to wriggle and jerk as if in an effort to raise the upper part of her body high enough to grasp the rope, but whether she was simply not strong or agile enough or whether she feared to dislodge her feet from the rings, she failed repeatedly to do this, and in the intervals she would hang upside down, her head sometimes twisted round so that she could see her partner, saying something to him over and over again that in the rising hubbub I could not catch. He for his part was hauling and pulling and jerking at the rope in a manner that seemed to impede her efforts to grasp it and perhaps endangered the precarious tenure her feet had of their rings.

"How long this first part of her contretemps lasted I do not know, but during it in any case I began to feel a sensation hitherto unknown to me, and hitherto, in terms of pleasurable sensation, without compare.

"She wore a red custume in two pieces, one in which encased her breasts and the other her nether parts; and when she jerked herself forward and upward in her endeavours to catch the rope with her hands I could see the articulation of the vertebrae in her lower back. When on the other hand she desisted in her efforts and hung helplessly upside down facing us I could see the skin tauten over her rib cage and the hollowing of her stomach as she gasped. I remember being especially taken, if that is the phrase, by the underside of her chin when she hung fully upside down, by the contractual motions her throat occasionally made as if she were swallowing, by her opened lips with their glimpse of inner, unpainted cutaneous tissue and by the inside of her thighs.

"After some time she ceased her wriggling and jerking attempts to catch the rope and simply hung there, her eyes closed, her arms hanging, her hands clenching and unclenching. Her companion however continued to agitate the rope violently in an effort to free it and he had done this perhaps five or six times after she had ceased her own efforts when she began to shout. Each time he jolted the rope she would let out a yell. The noise she emitted seemed to me like a cry for help, but it may not have been, for the whole place was now in an uproar. Whatever caused them anyway, a desire for succour or bodily distress, these almost rhythmic shouts increased my involuntary excitement.

"The ring master now appeared with two or three attendants and all began to haul and jerk spasmodically and, I am afraid, confusedly at the rope. Apparently as a result of some especially violent haul or jerk, one of her feet was displaced from its ring so that she hung by one foot and leg only."

"Not many feet from where you sat," gasped Riley.

"Precisely my dear fellow. And she now began to scream. A sort of high wail or ululation came from her lips as she hung there, repeated over and over again and ending in a sort of gasp. This was accompanied each time by a kicking motion of her free leg, a backward and forward thrashing, possibly the result of mere panic, perhaps designed to restore the foot to its ring. It of course greatly increased her danger as even I, in a sense unconcerned as I was, could see. Her companion now left the end of the rope in other hands, rushed forward and standing beneath her with his arms spread out either in supplication or preparedness began to speak. His words apparently had some effect for she ceased the violent and dangerous motion of the freed leg and allowed it to hang awkwardly, bent at the knee, away from its fellow. As a result perhaps of this, my attention became concentrated on the upper part of her thighs, where they conjoined with her torso and on the cloth stretched over that part of her anatomy which separated them; and as she hung there, rhythmically shrieking, I experienced for the first time, in a series of spasms accompanying her yells, that most intense of all bodily pleasures, the one which the creator perhaps deserves most credit for creating, if create it he did, in spite of all the trouble it has caused us." He produced his red-spotted handkerchief again and dabbed his eyes. "Ah dear, dear me," he said, "the days that are no more. And sorrow's crown of sorrow is remembering happier things."

Susan was now crouched on the floor of the attic, her hair sometimes held back by one hand, at others a dark curtain over her face, examining some photographs which showed pretty girls of another era being made to suffer in ingenious ways.

Some of these females were altogether naked, some in various states of undress like herself. There was one photograph in particular over which she lingered for a little while. It showed an altogether naked and somewhat sulky beauty suspended from above by the wrists, her breasts elevated and flattened by the position of her arms; and as she looked at it she felt a curious thrill, compounded of pity and trepidation, but not unmixed with pleasure.

The lecturer was silent for a moment. His auditors waited in vain.

"Would you mind telling us," asked Riley, "how did they get her down?"

"What? Oh, yes. They brought a ladder. They brought a ladder and some of them held it bolt upright with its top in the air. It took a little while and watching the way she managed to get a grip and the way she eventually fell to the ground and was picked up and assisted from the ring by many willing hands, provided, if I may say so, a pleasant decrescendo, a thing that is very necessary on these occasions if what I might call a stark anti-climax, the well-known sudden *tristesse* is to be avoided. I was now much concerned about the possibility that my excitements and their result might have come to the notice of my parents who were sitting on either side of me. Because their attention was likewise concentrated on her, however—doubtless out of human anxiety for her safety—on my mother's part anyway—they did not notice that anything out of the ordinary had occurred where I was concerned. Fortunately I was wearing long pants. It is the custom to put little boys into long pants for the first time on the occasion of their confirmation. A good old custom. I should be sorry to see it go."

"Of course," said Riley. "The old customs are best. The old folk knew that. But what is the moral of the story? What is the psycho-sexual nub of the matter?"

"It will cause me pain to elaborate on it, and I think indeed men of your perception might have grasped the matter by now, but here goes.

"I have ever been susceptible to beauty, all the wild summer in its most fleeting smile, and as I grew up I was frequently lovelorn. For the objects of my passion, for such I suppose it was, I cherished none but feelings of tenderness and wonder. I longed to prove myself in their eyes in ways other than as a mere manipulator of their persons to give pleasure. Indeed I rehearsed situations of romantic advantage within myself as other youths rehearse situations of sexual advantage. Perhaps however because of the very intensity of my wishes I never got *en rapport* with any of the causes of my heart's soarings, and so the question of any physical relationship with them never actually arose. Because of the pressure to conform that we all feel in adolescence, however, I had to pretend that like everybody else I was intent on sexual advantage; and because of my then obvious attractions I was frequently put in a position where I was enabled to make at least fumbling efforts to take it. Maybe for the reason that the girls who—shall I say it?—fell within my grasp, were not in themselves very attractive and I was ever fastidious, the experiences I had, mostly it is true confined to the initial stages of courtship, were not noticeable for their erotic intensity. Indeed, not to put too fine a point on it, they were dead-sea fruit.

"The intense experiences that I did have were mostly of a mental nature. I had and have a strong imagination. They were not, though, about physical contacts between myself and others. I imagined seeing girls, partially clothed, in circumstances of pain or difficulty, and among these many imaginings that of the female acrobat was a recurrent one.

"Well, due to the pressures of my baccalaureate, to the fact that my romantic affections were always hopelessly but intensely engaged elsewhere and that I have a large degree of timidity in my nature, I remained a virgin until after I went to Downing to take my master's and subsequently my doctorate. There I was smitten by an English girl, a blonde English rose. As we all know, English girls are different."

Riley and the Baron nodded grave assent.

"They will not take no for an answer. Lovelorn though I was, she gently and unobtrusively led me to the point of no return. I made my first full conquest. Well, we were happy for a while and I derived I think an almost ordinary degree of satisfaction from palpitations, agglutinations and conjunctions of a broadly orthodox kind. However, after some time she left me. I do not know why. Perhaps I was too busy with my doctorate. In any case in the fullness of time and the ordinary course of events there were others. English girls also, if not always roses. It must have been during the third or perhaps the fourth temporary liaison that I began to feel there was something unsatisfactory for me in ordinary sexual converse. I began to think back. I do not know the etiology of my wishes, whether they were born in babyhood out of the blessed flower of innocence, and perhaps far pre-dated the advent of the girl in the circus tent, but in any case it seems to me that she, so to speak, pin-pointed them."

"You are therefore a living example of the inefficacy of censorship," contributed the Baron.

"I dare say, but in any case to cut a long story short, it gradually grew upon me over the years and during subsequent relationships that I only found true delight in certain circumstances, and that through the medium of certain acquiescences on the part of my partner which are by no means easy to come by."

He lowered his voice again, so that even the barmen paused in their work to listen; and the whole pub was silent. "It dawned upon me in short," he said, "that I only found true delight when the girl was in a predicament, a position of disadvantage and distress."

Riley chortled. "But isn't that the normal and approved position?" he enquired.

She was wondering if many men were ... that way inclined. There was often a bit of rough stuff, of course. Come to think of it, some men did a bit more slapping you and pinching you and pushing you about than others. Of course some were just bastards and liked to throw their weight about. Not to mind the way that Timbo had of pushing her head down with his hand on the back of her neck. And a couple of times he had held her head there while he came in her mouth, which he knew she didn't like. Ugh. She had had a good mind to bite it.

141

Generally speaking, thought the Baron, strolling along the north side of St Stephen's Green again on the way to his appointment with the Minister, it is a mistake for a poor man to associate with those richer than himself. The hope of a successful touch will make every moment of the converse, unknown to the other party, an expense of spirit in a waste of momently advanced remorse and foolishness, for if everything hangs on the possibility of success, a desperate man will babble endlessly on instead of coming to the point. If he has any money he is liable to spend it in the initial stages of converse in order to conceal for a while his secret motive. Then, perhaps, pride takes over from hesitency; the tears that lead one's companions in poverty to empty their pockets on the table are never shed, and in any case the rich would fly in embarrassment from them if they were. Nor, so relative were the definitions of poverty and affluence in this world, was it ever plausible to hope that the richer party's perceptions would lead them to make an offer. In the present case it was undoubtedly true that the Minister knew him to be broke or thereabouts, but what was his definition of that state? Did he know him to be destitute?

He did a pocket count. He had five and fourpence ha'penny. It was a quarter to one. The appointment was for one o'clock, and if he was there first he would have to buy himself a drink, not to say offer the Minister one. He was forty-eight years of age; he was, in his own sphere, moderately well-known; and this was the kind of calculation he had to make on the way to an appointment with a contemporary.

Things were bad, there was no doubt about it. Even if he got free of this awful trap he was in, what the hell was he going to do? Work would not save him, circumstantially anyway, that was for sure. But in any case what chance had he of doing any work? Even supposing he didn't go to gaol? He thought of Susan, who had sold the contents of the box to a London manuscript dealer. In conjunction with a boy-friend, he had no doubt about that, probably a pot-bellied folk-musician, or a bearded proletarian playwright. They had put their heads together and sold the proofs of his ancestry. He had absolutely no doubt.

It was true that Riley had not found out anything from the other bloody dealer. "His humanity did not take precedence over his occupation," Riley had said. "He actually had the face to say that there were unwritten rules about not asking questions unless there was a bona fide reason, but that in any case his London colleague would never disclose the source. The only circumstance in which he would disclose the source to another dealer would be if they had reason to believe there was deception which might affect them both.

"But I'll tell you something else. Do you know what he said the stuff might be worth on the face of it? Two thousand quid. At first he wouldn't say anything at all: then he said if there was a real cache of related matter, including Parnell letters of any importance, it would be worth at least two thousand quid. I asked about Joyce letters and he laughed. He pointed out that there was no mention of Joyce letters but he said that if there were any—of interest, as he put it—he wouldn't care to put a price on it at all. Astronomical, he said. It seems to me, old boy, that when you sold the—what shall we say?—counterfeited matter for a mere six hundred saucepan lids you sold yourself considerably short. Astronomical indeed. Of course when I mentioned Joyce letters he was considerably baffled; and I do believe for a while he thought I was simply ignorant of the dates of the gentlemen in question; that I had Parnell writing to Joyce or vice versa. I left him to his bafflement, though. Whatever he thinks he can go on thinking it."

And so they had parted, with, among other last words, an exhortation on Riley's part to "ask that bloody girl of yours about it. Ask her straight out—tell her the whole thing. If she put the stuff into the dealer's hands she can get it back. It seems to me you don't know your strength with her at all. For God's sake find out from her what the score is anyway. While there's life there's hope you know."

But there bloody well wasn't. He was dished, well and truly dished. He was involved in a sordid and complicated piece of deception with an element of the ridiculous in it which had now been increased; and, apart from anything else, Susan and her proletarian playwright were probably just now laughing at him behind his back. He was all alone, a ridiculous figure with no hope for the future and a very real possibliity of going to gaol, forty-eight years of age and a failure as painter even if only by virtue of the fact that he could no longer paint, at present plodding along the Green twenty minutes early for an appointment which would merely be a resumption of a totally implausible and profitless acquaintanceship.

"Hi!"

He wheeled about. A tall boy in jeans, a blue shirt and a sort of sailor's pea-jacket stood smiling at him from the edge of the pavement. Beside him was a girl, also in jeans and shirt but without the jacket. Her shirt, the Baron noted, had pockets which buttoned down over her breasts. He extended his hand, formally, ridiculously, continental fashion.

"I saw your show," he said. "I liked those things very much. I really did."

The boy said nothing. They gazed at each other, humorously, affectionately, a little anxiously on both sides. The Baron felt constrained to say something more.

"Lot of work in it," he said.

"Yes, I've been very active," said the other.

"No I didn't mean that," said the Baron. "I meant that kind of thing—those sort of things—involve a lot of work."

"Where are you off to?" the other asked, still smiling, not being forthcoming about the stupid remark the Baron had just made.

"Well, er, I'm going to have lunch with a Minister of State, actually. There." He gestured towards the pink and white frontage of the Shelbourne.

The other turned to the smiling girl. "The Baron's lunching with the mighty," he said. "Isn't that a gas?"

"The company we keep," said the girl.

The remark wasn't much, thought the Baron, but in her English accent it sounded sort of bright. They were making, he thought, a little too much of it. They probably lunched with people every day in the week. They shone with activity, private money, critical acclaim, sexual adjustment, youth and confidence. A curious contrast to my sorry self, he thought. But he knew things this chap would never know.

"Have you time for a drink? We're only round the corner as you know. I've got a drop of some filthy gin or other that some mutt brought to a party and Anna's always complaining that you never come to see us. Besides, I want to show you something."

"Just about," said the Baron. He was immensely fond of this chap, but so far the encounter wasn't doing him any good at all. Still, he might as well go for a drink. He found the girl attractive, even though he had a feeling that she fancied herself a little bit too much and thought she didn't have to say anything in consequence. And he might, he just might, touch them for a pound before he went on his way. That would solve any problem that could be posed if the Minister was late and he had to wait in the bar.

As they went into the little kitchen the Baron said: "You know what it reminds me of? It reminds me a bit of the toy railway you used to have up in the attic in Loudon Road."

They both laughed.

"Where would you show a thing like that?" the Baron asked.

"Nowhere that I know of really," the other said. "In the United States they loan the lucky people big rooms in the permanent galleries for that sort of thing."

"Where would it go eventually? Permanently I mean?"

"It would go in a public gallery if it had a room or a sort of alcove to itself. Bother galleries, though. I wouldn't like to think of it as a museum object."

"Bother them indeed."

"It would go in a private house too if somebody had a spare empty room they could put it into. Go and look at it now and then. Like the old toy railway. To hell with houses too though."

"Up to a point," said the Baron. "I wouldn't mind having one again actually."

"You will, of course. Won't they do something for you."

"Who's they might I ask?"

"Oh damn it, Richard. Somebody. Some of your smart

friends."

"You must remember," said the Baron, "that we're operating in an Irish context. A penniless man never gets anything. It's the old story. I need capital." He laughed. "For my railway systems."

The boy betrayed hesitency. "Where are you staying at the moment then?" he asked.

"I've got a loan of his place from Jonathen Edwards. for a couple of weeks." The Baron finished his drink and put the glass down on the spotlessly scrubbed oil-cloth. He was conscious of the girl looking at him. She fancies me a bit, too, he thought. Always has done. Old soldier. To change the subject he said: "You seem pretty snug here."

"Yep. The house belongs to young Wexford and I don't pay any rent. There never seems to be anybody in the rest of it, does there, Anna?

"Never," the girl said in the tone of slight English wonder she brought to many things.

As if further explanation was needed the boy added: "Anna has a part-time job and I make a bit now and then. This used to be all one big attic I think. Then somebody partitioned it up. I knocked one of the partitions out to make the studio. It's nice being right under the roof, though of course it's a nuisance being at the top of a house. You know, you have to lug big things up and down."

"I'd better go," the Baron said. It was a long time since he had lugged anything up or down.

"I'll come with you," the boy said. On the stairs he added: "Mother wants you to write to her."

"Oh." He couldn't react. "Has she been writing to me?" he asked.

"Apparently."

"Well I haven't been getting any letters."

And as they went on down he thought: I have another problem. I'll have to tell him something about this sordid and ridiculous thing I've got myself into. Of course he was only a stepson, so if there was any publicity it cast no nasturtiums whatever on his actual ancestry. Was he still a stepson, or did that relationship cease when the marriage ... broke up?

146

At the door, in Frederick Street, the Baron said: "Have you got any money?"

"Yeh, I'm O.K. for the time being. That commission I got for the insurance company building ... " He stopped suddenly, blushing. "Oh good God ... I'm sorry .... I misunderstood. I've got some here ...." He dug in his pocket, producing a pound and some small change. "Anna's got some more upstairs," he said. "And we've got some in the bank."

He's really kind of English, the Baron thought. Or Anglo or something. And smart. Sort of London smart. They survived. If they had any problems they contrived that they were explainable and wouldn't really disgrace them.

"No, the pound will do fine," he said, picking it out. "Just so that I have money in my pocket when I meet his nibs."

But as far as beating and whipping and that sort of thing was concerned? Of course a lot of them might want to but knew they couldn't get away with it. Unless you were a prisoner in a concentration camp or something ... .

Her own da, she thought, had been a bit fond of the physical punishment side of things.

She remembered that time in the cold kitchen, trying to get away from him, pulling down her inadequate little vest and getting whacks from the cane on the thighs and knuckles. And even years later, when she was thirteen or fourteen, he had whacked her on the behind with his belt in the bedroom ... . Though he didn't in fact make her take off her skirt, not like Joan O'Mara's da, the brute. According to Joan anyway.

There had of course been that producer fellow in London that Irene had introduced her to, if producer he was. The one with the lovely big flat in St John's Wood and the bedroom with the Soulages paintings. "Actually what I had in mind was a bit of swishing, love," he had said. And then what was it? "No, no, my dear. You have it wrong. I'm not actually much of a whippee. More of a whipper, in fact." But he was only like a lot of other men in the end and had turned all creepy and miserable when she'd laughed at him. Up to that point she really had thought he was a masterful enough sort of fellow ... .

147

If the truth were known, once or twice since she had imagined the scene with him sort of different and with a different sort of ... well ... ending. Not that she had any intention in the world of ever letting anybody lay into her, with a leather or anything else. Not in a million years.

She was an attractive wench, that one, the Baron thought, walking up Kildare Street in the sunlight. But together they were sort of neutral ... no ... perhaps dimorphic was the word. As if there wasn't enough difference between them for the last bit of fun to be extracted from things.

Is it some sort of innocence, some sort of Garden of Eden thing they all have, or am I just getting older, so that they seem like children?

No, it wasn't innocence they had, he thought, walking again past the Guinness archbishop. Freshness, hope, naturalness, yes. But innocence, no. He was the one who had that commodity, "a sort of battered kettle at the heel". It belonged to him and his like, this special kind of innocence. It was a mark of age. You had to be born in the old world to possess it. Like all marks of age it should imply honour, but of course what it implied was a capacity for dishonour. For retreat, concealment, perversion. Only he and his like really had that. A capacity for the perversion of innocence. They had the open thing. He had the closed.

But they were in fact nice works of art that Patrick was making. It was nice too that everybody had broken out and was having fun, in sort of painting-cum-sculpture anyway, though of course he was more tolerant where that sort of thing was concerned. Not like me, he thought, with my dull, dark exactitudes, my meticulous, analytic, almost guilt-laden brush. Still there had to be some agony in it or it wasn't any good. An agony of exactitude. There should be some assertion of freedom too, though. Some gestures of release from the beginning, not just a kind of disemburdening at the end. "You're too accurate, too analytic," Myles had said to him years ago, standing in front of his flower pots, in the old studio in Hatch Lane, with the belt of the raincoat hanging down and the hat on his head. "You're too much the bloody Jesuit framing a definition, altogether too scrupulous. You should let yourself go. Do something outrageous, shocking. Let it rip. Stop caring so much about the world of appearances."

Well, he had thought it bad advice and he never had stopped caring about the world of appearances. He never had let it rip. He had always tried to contain things, to describe them with fanatical scrupulosity, and perhaps the necessary anxieties of precision had made the ultimate spirit of the work dull. Well, he couldn't help that.

Certainly, taking it all together—and for an instant, walking along, he saw some of the old familiar, too familiar paintings—he had hoped to be past this kind of thing by now, out of his cage, not necessarily into some kind of abstraction, but into some area of freedom or other. He thought of his planks, his planes, his nine hundred angles of vision. Damn them. However necessary. Or satisfying.

When and if he did break out though, what had gone before might stand him in good stead. You should not break out until you could bear the confinement no longer. Then you could properly take advantage of freedom, utilising all the dirty prison tricks you had learned. And make a mockery out of your voluntary abnegations in the past, for which of course nobody had ever given you credit, probably putting them down to incurable poverty of spirit.

Humanly you should do that too. Break out. Get free. Get money. Get Susan.

"Your friend Pigott," said the Minister, slowly, deliberately.

"Oh yes?" said the Baron. At last it had come.

"I take it you know the bones of the story?"

The Baron nodded.

"He was an unsavoury character," said the Minister. "Most unsavoury. He operated under false names, did you know that?"

The Baron took a little gulp of his Irish coffee and nodded.

"Ponsonby was one of them. Ronald Ponsonby."

The Minister looked the Baron straight in the eye. "He called himself Ponsonby, Ponsonby," he said.

The Baron said nothing. "Oh well," said the Minister. "He also called himself De Vere, Arbuthnot, Montmorency, not to mention Smith and Brown."

There was a pause.

"At least you don't do that," said the Minister. "I'll say that for you. To the best of my knowledge and belief you have never called yourself Montmorency or Smith. Let's hope you never will."

The Baron smiled, perhaps a trifle wanly.

"You know about the Loyal and Patriotic Union which provided the money for the Parnell letters, I suppose," continued the Minister. "It was really one of those old womanish witch-hunting organisations which are familiar everywhere, but which were perhaps most familiar in the United States in our time. They are financed by rich hysterics, run by idiots and exploited by crooks. This one was run by a certain Edward Caulfield Houston, an idiot if ever there was one. Pigott was simply a crook who exploited it. Small blame to him.

"He did Parnell a good turn, if anything, in the process. Incidentally there is a note on the file which suggests that certain elements among the Fenians may have been aware of what he was up to, and rather approved." He paused. "I don't know why I'm telling you all this," he said.

The Baron gestured.

"You also know I take it that Pigott sold his patriotic journals to a company in which Parnell held the majority of the shares as trustee of the Land League."

The Baron nodded. He did know.

The Minister toyed with the stem of his glass, frowning. He appeared to find what he had to say next distasteful. "There is a full report of this transaction on the file," he said, "and there are also various notes that could refer to it. 'It seems that P will not meet P's price'—that sort of thing. 'Chief baulking at the amount asked' and so forth. But some of them might not refer to that transaction at all. Or else there was more to that transaction than meets the eye. The trouble is that whoever

150

was in charge of this file was a bit of a joker. He had a happy little playground of his own and he had some joke up his sleeve. Do you get me? He knew something that doesn't appear specifically on the file but that he seems to be referring to."

He paused for a moment, lost in thought, still fiddling with the stem of his glass. "There need be nothing unusual about that," he went on. "If the fellow who kept the file never had occasion to submit a formal written report about this other matter, whatever it was, it wouldn't necessarily appear on the file anyway. Whether or no he had communicated it verbally to his superiors there might be only references to it. Do you understand?"

The Baron nodded uncertainly. He only understood up to a point.

"There were other transactions, or an other transaction. Monetary. Between the Chief and Pigott. Do you get me?"

The Baron nodded. He had thought so.

"Dammit, don't you see? He was blackmailing him."

"What about?" asked the Baron.

"I don't know," said the Minister. "And if I did I wouldn't tell you. This doesn't concern just Pigott. It concerns Parnell, who's always hot news. And you're too bloody indiscreet. Besides, you're a romantic. It's better for you not to know. After all the Chief is a great romantic hero. I know a lot of things you don't know and that might keep you awake at night if you did. Let this be one of them."

He eyed the Baron humorously over the rim of his glass. "We mustn't destroy your romantic picture of him," he said.

"Was it sexual?" asked the Baron anxiously.

The Minister nodded. "So far as I can make out, it was," he said.

"To do with Mrs O'Shea?" asked the Baron tensely.

"Arrah, not at all," said the Minister. "From the time it began—and it didn't begin until quite late in the day, mind you—the Kitty O'Shea thing was known to all and sundry. Bugger that. You're being stupid now. There was only one person it was necessary to keep the Kitty O'Shea thing from and that was Aunt Ben. Everybody else knew all about it. Even Gladstone knew, and a Prime Minister, let me assure you, is always the last to know about anything. Have some sense man. It was ... something else."

"What?" asked the Baron point blank.

"I have told you I don't bloody well know," said the Minister. "And I have also said that if I did I wouldn't tell you. But look here. Parnell was thirty-four when he met Kitty O'Shea. Well, hell's bells man, use your common sense. A fellow doesn't come to the age of thirty-four without getting up to something. It's the same with all the great Victorians. The big romance diverts attention from other matters. Perhaps it's even meant to. Browning was thirty-four when he ran away with Miss Barrett. They must have been up to something beforehand. These anchorites, they usually are up to something, dammit, you know, they often have, or acquire, strongly marked preferences. They often have funny preferences to begin with, these solitary fellows. That's why they are solitaries. And then there's all that freedom to ... experiment."

"Yes," said the Baron. "And imagine."

"What's that? Oh well, I suppose so, but most well-to-do fellows in Victorian times didn't have to do much imagining. Don't have to in any old times if it comes to that. As you would know if you knew anything about the world you live in."

"H'mm," said the Baron. "So you think Pigott may have known something about the Chief's ... preferences or practices and have been putting the screws on him."

"I didn't say I thought anything of the kind," said the Minister sternly. "I said the fellow who kept the file may have thought so, or may have known so, or thought he knew so. Personally I wouldn't have bet on getting very far with that kind of thing where Parnell was concerned. Or indeed with any kind of sexual blackmail where anybody was concerned in Victorian times. But your Mr Pigott was a strange fellow and God knows what he knew or thought he knew—and, if it comes to that, what sort of a use he may have threatened to make of it.

"He certainly knew a lot about people's preferences, though, because for one thing he flogged pictures, dirty pictures. Photographs. Some of them he apparently took himself, others he imported from the Rue D'Alsace. The camera was new then, newer than it is now anyway, though of course it's still only in its infancy and we haven't measured the full effects of our ability to reproduce images of ourselves at will yet. Anyway its possibilities in that line were then a pleasing novelty, which some bright boys, and girls too I daresay, were on to. Mr Pigott had a large and varied clientele for his pictures, including almost the whole blooming membership of the Royal St George Yacht Club, Kingstown—to which, I may say, I have the honour to belong, and to which he belonged himself. Its then President, Lord Muskerry, was a particularly good client or warm patron, whichever you like to call it. Democracy, technology and the breakdown of morality are only beginning to bring such delights to the masses now, but Pigott's patrons were mostly members of the upper classes; and even the postal traffic he conducted was a select one. Accordingly the fellows who arranged the photographs were able to cater for certain human leanings in a way the proprietors of these new pictorial magazines we hear about are not, or probably, in view of certain public considerations, ever will be; and among the most interesting of Mr Pigott's photographs are representations of young females being subjected to various forms of torment and ill-usage, some of them rather ingenious.

"For the traffic in these photographs he used yet another name. Greene. Martin R. Greene; and the names of a great many of his postal clients are on the file. The Chief's is not among them. The kind of thing represented was probably in line with his own preferences, because it seems that whenever our friend went abroad he went indefatigably to the sort of establishment which was known to the police as a 'house of abuse'. That rather quaint name designated one where you could engage in, or at least witness, a bit of whipping or whatnot. Some of this carry-on was mere theatre, as you can probably surmise. Some of it was real enough, God help us, the girls being unlucky victims who had been procured through the slave traffic and were kept as prisoners for the purpose of having the lard beaten out of them. There was such a place in London where he went, and there was also one in Brighton.

The Chief was fond of Brighton, as you probably know, but let's not jump to conclusions.

"There was one especially notorious place in Lyons which our friend was very fond of visiting. It was stocked by slavers using North Africa as a source of supply. Some quite extreme forms of ill-usage of the girls was said to be permitted to the customers there, though in my own humble opinion it would take a lot to exceed what women will inflict on themselves. Anyway, the existence of this place seems to have been the main reason why our friend visited Lyons at all, which he did rather frequently when he was living high off the hog on the monies provided by the Loyal and Patriotic. He stayed in Lyons at the Hotel Bristol."

Here the Minister paused. "Under the name Ponsonby," he added sternly. The Baron said nothing. "Ronald Ponsonby," said the Minister.

The Baron continued to say nothing.

"Oh come off it, Dicky. My powers of deduction are not what they were, but when you asked me to interest myself in Mr Pigott on your behalf I couldn't help putting two and two together. I remember a certain occasion in Knockley College when one or other of us was said to be of the Clan Pigott. I knew it must be one or other of us two, since we were the only people in the whole bloody place who had any tinge of distinction or consequence about them. That this was due to our talents, so nebulous and yet so unmistakeable, I was prepared to admit, but I suspected also that there was a dash of blood in your case. When in after years I heard you had changed your name by deed poll I was both amused and admiring. The fact that you adopted a nom de guerre at the same time rather puzzled me. I should have thought Richard Pigott would have been a perfectly splendid name to paint and, if I may put it that way without offence, to operate under. However, I can see now that there was a point in that too. Dashing. Very dashing indeed. Ponsonby. There's only one thing."

"What's that?" asked the Baron.

"There's more on the file than I've told you. And if you believe, as I believe you believe, that you are Richard Pigott's grandson, and if you're banking anything on that belief, which, if I may say so, I believe you are, then you'd better know."

"Oh for God's sake yes," said the Baron.

"When he shot himself in Madrid he had two sons."

·"I was aware of that," said the Baron.

"Their names were changed and they were sent to Knockley College."

"I knew that too."

"Now oddly enough—or perhaps not oddly—there is no mention of the new names on the file. This may have been evidence of humanity on the part of those who compiled it, or maybe the Castle just didn't know. Perhaps it didn't care. But there was in fact a custom that when a new life was begun—say by some wretched informer or other who had been shipped off to the colonies—the memorandum of his new identity and whereabouts was actually abstracted from the file and destroyed after fifteen years if all had gone well. Puff. Like that" —he clicked his fingers—"up in smoke. A curiously fairminded people in some deluded ways, the British. And it is just possible that the same rule was applied to these two little chisellers in their late Victorian knickerbockers. That would mean that somewhere around 1903 all reference to them would have been abstracted and destroyed. Do you follow me?"

The Baron nodded. He did.

"But it wasn't. Or not quite all. That's the strange thing. And," said the Minister slowly, "whatever you fancy your connection with either of those lads to be you had better perhaps know that there are in fact two notes, sort of addenda to the file and made in a hand which doesn't previously appear there. One of them says, 'W.P., died Chimo, Ungava Bay, Labrador Peninsula, Province of Quebec, Canada, December 28th 1910'." He paused for a moment, as if to allow this to sink in, and then he continued, "The other says, 'R.P. died Dublin, Ireland, August 12th 1915'."

He paused again. The Baron was silent. "1915. That would seem to rule you out," the Minister quietly said. "Unless of course you were a gin fed, artificially stunted, beardless wonder in Knockley College in the years we both remember. But as it happens I didn't rest there. I thought I'd check first on

155

the Dublin R.P., but then it struck me, which of course is true, that the Dublin R.P. would be vastly the more difficult one of the two. I didn't know what Fort Chimo might amount to, but I imagined that it was likely to be a smaller place than Dublin, and one whose records had been subject to less hazards, in peace and in war, than our own poor lot. So I got on to the Canadians. It seems there was a W.P. who died in Fort Chimo, in the province of Quebec on the date in question. As a matter of fact the whole of that vast Dominion knew about his death before the matter was over and done with; and there were certainly people who wished he'd never been born. To cut a long story short, Mr W. P. was a ne'er do well who arrived in Fort Chimo about nineteen hundred and seven. For one reason or another the place was comparatively populous and prosperous at the time, and full of drifters like himself. He kept a bar for a while and, according to the police, may have been a procurer of sorts—supplying Indian or Eskimo women, whichever kind they have there, for rough-necks and roustabouts like himself. Then it appears he actually married a native woman. He paid the proper price for her and everything was done according to the satisfaction of her tribe and relatives, but it seems he maltreated her, and he went on maltreating her, in spite of their protests, until eventually they killed him. The police tried to apprehend the murderers and there was some fighting in which three policemen were killed, as well as a number of members of Mrs W. P.'s tribe. He was a bad egg, our Mr W. P., and he certainly made his name well enough known after he died, for the affair dragged on endlessly, and there was a lot of blood on the snow before it was finished."

He paused. "The name in question was Power, William Power," he said and paused again. "Your name was Power," he added, gently enough.

The Baron nodded.

"And that would seem to confirm something," the Minister said. "Though what it is you want confirmed I don't know."

"All right," said the Baron. "There were only two sons. I believe myself to be the son of one of them. You've told me about the adventurer of the family. Now what about the stay-at-home? If the official who made the note was keeping tabs on the Pigott boys and if he was right about the other one dying in 1915, that, as you so succinctly put it, rules me out. Did he? Did an R. Power—a Richard Power—die in Dublin in 1915? My father's name was Richard, and so to the best of my knowledge and belief was the younger Pigott boy's. I believe them in fact to have been one and the same person, but my father died in 1918, in the war to end all wars."

"It's difficult to say," said the Minister, "because a considerable part of that year, including the date in question, went up in smoke when the Public Record Office was malafoostered in 1922. A lot of the deaths are missing. If this R.P. was R. Power and if he had property and made a will we would know; but the puzzle remains because whereas two R. Powers, a Richard and a Robert, did die in the city of Dublin in 1915 after having made testamentary dispositions on which probate was granted, neither of them died on the date in question and neither of them was Richard Pigott's son. We can assume that because neither of them ever suffered a name change. You've been into the question of the name change yourself, I hope?"

The Baron nodded again. "In so far as I was able," he said.

"Well, I'm abler than you," said the Minister, "and I've been into it too. It's funny, but there's no record of the Pigott boys' name change. Not in 1889, and not at any stage later. And there should be a record. It seems as if somebody was bending the rules again. It wasn't much different under the British you know. An Archbishop could more or less get what he wanted; Pigott had done the Raj a few good turns; and so Bob was your Uncle. Or not as the case might be."

There was another long pause. "I'm afraid you'll have to take it that the fellow who made the note knew his stuff," said the Minister then. "After all he was right about Fort Chimo, and that's a long way away. Why shouldn't he be right about something nearer home?"

The Baron nodded automatically. He had had another series of shocks. Was there going to be nothing left to him at all?

"There's one other little thing," the Minister added then,

"but I don't know if it's of any significance and I only mention it because after I'd been sitting there looking at that note on the file for a little while it began to bother me. The note itself is signed "R.P.". It's peculiar, but it is. At first I thought that what came after the entry was "R.I.P." and that it had been added by somebody with a sense of what was fitting or somebody with a sense of humour. But no. It says, "W.P. died Fort Chimo" et cetera. "R.P. died Dublin, Ireland, August 12th 1915. R.P. August 12th 1915." The fellow who added the note had the same initials and he took care to put them on record."

The Parnell letters and the other stuff hadn't meant much to her. Although she knew a bit about Irish history, she didn't fully understand the context. It was just beginning to dawn on her, though, that there were a lot of R.P.'s about. There was Ronald or Roddy Ponsonby, whom she knew, though evidently not as well as she had thought, not by any means. There was Richard Power, the nephew of the house she was in, more than likely the boy in the first communion photographs and the same fellow as Mr Roddy Ponsonby or she was a Dutchman. Some of Mr Ponsonby's friends even called him Richard or Dickey. And now there was this Richard Pigott of the box and the nasty photographs, a shadowy, indistinct figure from her previous knowledge of history, but judging from the contents of the box, quite a card. And Mr Ponsonby was quite a card too.

The Minister had waited till they were seated at a table in the Shelbourne's rather ornate, Edwardian dining room, having mutually disdained various local variants of well-known French dishes and jointly ordered oxtail soup, roast beef, roast potatoes and green peas. Then he had put the tips of his fingers together and gazed sternly across the table at the Baron.

"Those letters you wrote me," he said. "Last Christmas or whenever it was. Don't ever write me letters like that again."

The Baron had said nothing.

"I don't want to hear about your troubles," the Minister had said. "I have troubles enough of my own." He paused. "And I have a particular distaste for being either bullied or ... blackmailed. Do you get me?"

The Baron had started to say something, but the Minister silenced him with an upraised palm. "Fortunately," he said, "I found them rather obscure. I have still no idea whether you were merely suggesting that I had a moral obligation to help, having led you on with some sort of promises in the past; or whether you were implying that it would be the worse for me if I didn't. And whichever it was, I don't want any elucidation now. It was the wrong approach. Let's leave it at that."

The Baron made a gesture which he hoped implied assent. He was quite glad to leave it at that. But the Minister was not quite finished with the subject. "In any case," he had said, "there was—there is—damn all I can do. I'm a very, very poor man myself these days, I can assure you."

The Baron had breathed a sigh of relief. That disposed of that possibility anyway. He could now proceed to enjoy himself after a fashion. A touch at least was out.

The Minister smiled at him, man to man, conspiratorially, across the table. The Baron's relief was mingled with that strange sense of warmth radiated all round which he had often felt before in the present company. What a strange gift, he thought. Magnetism. Did I once have something like it myself, before my ... troubles came upon me?

"And I hear you're in trouble again now," the Minister was saying. "There's something I heard about you. Something about documents." He filled the Baron's glass and raised his own up to the light appreciatively. "You really are an extraordinary bloody man," he said.

"What throws me," he said, "is this extraordinary mixture of integrity and criminality."

"Me too," said the Baron.

"I mean hell's bells man, even if you adopt something like painting as a profession it's normal, it's essential to make accommodations of some sort. Your form of abnegation is not normal. You won't do a damn thing to get money in the ordinary way—won't look for commissions, won't paint what people want you to paint, gave up the bloody landscapes the minute they began to sell—but you still have these expensive tastes, and so you go and do something ludicrous that gets you into endless trouble, some bloody bit of criminality that hasn't even the virtue of being straightforward and easy to understand—like this present carry-on, the details of which I cannot remember and do not wish to be reminded of."

So he knew then, thought the Baron. "It was done out of pure need," he said, though that wasn't true.

"Ay, the need for a whiskey and a few big bets and maybe even a skirt or two, that I'll lay. You always had these expensive tastes, as I remember. The bottles of Spanish Sauternes in the dormitory at night and the suits bought from Burton's the Fifty Shilling Tailors."

"Burton's and the Fifty Shilling Tailors were two different shops," said the Baron.

"Matter a damn," replied the Minister. "You must have been the only fellow in the whole history of Knockley College that ever bought a suit of clothes for himself. Altogether extraordinary. And now you're the poorest fellow I know. It's not natural for a fellow of your temperament to be poor. Not seemly. And not bloody necessary either if you ask me."

"Other painters have been poor," said the Baron, though it almost choked him to say it.

"Not quite so poor. Not for a while back. Not since the twenties. Anybody as talented as you has got more money. And anybody who hasn't has chucked it. You alone will neither chuck it nor make accommodations as far as I can see. Get a rich wife or mistress or boy-friend; seek out commissions; if that won't work do something"—he made a complicated motion with his fork in the air—"different, something outrageous. Break out, so the people will notice you."

"You called, sir?" asked the waiter.

"No," said the Minister, "I did not. Not yet."

He dazzled the Baron with a few more brush-strokes. "Something that will make you fashionable and be fun for you as well. For the matter of that, why the hell don't you try to get out of it and get into something else. There's nothing here of course, no money in any ... er artistic activities in this bloody country. But lots of you fellows have made a go of it in England. You've been over there. Beats me why you ever came back. Lots of opportunities there. Films, television, et cetera ... Fellow with your talents. Really no opportunities here for anybody. Anybody at all."

He stared moodily about the dining room of the Shelbourne as if the possibilities that he had once expected had not materialised and he was inclined to blame the place. A waiter left a trolley and began to remove the plates.

"And what can I get you to follow sir? We have ... ."

"Ice cream," said the Minister, a little petulantly. "Plain vanilla ice cream."

"Anything for you sir?" the waiter asked the Baron. "Cheese board sir?"

"An Irish coffee," said the Baron. "Double the whiskey."

"Damn good idea," said the Minister, brightening a bit. "I'll have one too."

"You know, my dear Baron," he continued, "thinking back, trying to think back to what we were both like I have the feeling that the first glimmerings of what you insist on calling vocation in any man, is simply the consciousness of being an elite spirit who should be free in some way from the degrading conditions under which most lives are lived."

He looked the Baron in the eye once more and smiled hs conspirator's smile. "What I am talking about is a sort of consciousness of being exceptional that belongs to exceptional men," he said. "Getting elected, stabbing people like Lannigan in the back occasionally, money and popularity, these things confirm it, but you have it before you have them, before you do a damn thing, even make one of those socialistic speeches to the debating society that you were so good at. Power is like sex. Everybody wants it but not everybody gets the real glow out of it. You've got to have something inside you for that, something wicked perhaps ... a knowledge that one is ... it. Do you get me?"

"I get you," the Baron said drily. "The feeling is not confined to statesmen."

The coffees had come and the Minister took a voluptuous sip. His good humour seemed to have been entirely restored.

"Something surrounds you, a sort of promise in the air that you can even sense yourself. One possesses, even for oneself, a sort of glamour."

So you do too, thought the Baron, and, once upon a time, even occasionally nowadays ... .

"Now if you've got this feeling," the Minister said, "your first duty is to it, not to a particular kind of painting or the policies of the party or the efficiency of the postal system or anything else. This is a miraculous human thing and it's really all you've got. It will last for quite a while on very little sustenance, but it won't last forever. You need a little applause and encouragement ... . Glamour feeds on glamour you know."

He looked over his shoulder and lowered his voice. "You know what I mean dammit," he said. "The prize of beauty's shining eyes and whatnot."

"Hmm," said the Baron, thinking of Susan.

"So you've got to choose," said the Minister, "some mode of expression that keeps you bouyant ... floating ... a source of possibilities, something that's exciting to do and worth doing of course, but the merely worth doing done without applause, admiration, love, awe ... you get dull that way, the spirit of an exceptional man becomes embittered and ... his doggedness defeats itself because he ceases to be a source of excitement, of possibilities, to himself or others. Get me?"

"There have been lonely men," said the Baron.

"I know, I know," said the Minister, raising an imperious hand. "Van Gogh, Leopardi ... they had a brief creative period and they died comparatively young. Early forties at most."

"Cezanne," said the Baron.

The Minister looked over his shoulder again. He leaned forward conspiratorially. "Dull," he said. "Great, of course, we all know that, but at the same time meticulously, even elaborately, dull. Admit it."

The Baron did, in part.

"You're getting on, you know," said the Minister. "You're getting on. You're not in the first rapture of youth any longer.

This may happen to you unless you break out a bit, do something that gives you this sense of being ... well, dammit, glamorous, something that alerts people, makes their eyes shine when they look at you."

"It's not glamour I'm after any longer," said the Baron. "It's dignity."

"You're going the right way about it," said the Minister, "let me tell you that."

"I may in the end perhaps," said the Baron, "have the dignity of my achievement. From what does your dignity come?"

"From everybody I look at. Even my enemies. Even those who affect to think I'm just a thooramalown who can manipulate the vote. Almost everybody I look at kow tows to me in one way or another. I'm a success and conscious of it. They are to some degree failures. That's power. Can you say that?"

"Power," said the Baron. "Don't talk nonsense. Look out of the window there."

They gazed through the great bay windows of the Shelbourne at a green St Stephen's Green, around it the life of the streets.

"That's your material out there," he said. "Can you manipulate it as I can, sometimes, manipulate mine?" He thought of his unfinished canvas with a great longing, as a drowning man might think of a boat drifting beyond his reach. "A world-wide system of mere mechanical proliferation," he said, "utterly beyond your control. Drift and greed rule that, whose operations you may very slightly modify, though I doubt if you bother, democrat that you are. You can neither oppose it nor create anything in its place. But only in creation is power manifest."

The Minister gulped down the remains of his Irish coffee. He continued to stare through the window. Suddenly he began to quote softly.

> "Ah love could thou and I conspire
> To grasp this sorry scheme of things entire,
> Would we not shatter it to bits and then
> Re-mould it nearer to our hearts desire?"

163

Beyond the hideous unfinished new office block a further row of perfect Georgian houses was being demolished.

"That," said the Baron, "is precisely what somebody appears to be doing."

Susan had now decided it was time for her visit to the police station, and therefore time to put some clothes on. She had accordingly gone down to her own room, where, after taking off her dressing gown and nightdress, she had stood for a little while, beautiful, young and naked, in front of the mirror on the back of the wardrobe door.

"And," said the Minister gently enough, "that would seem to dispose of the ancestral mansions, the Pigott connection, whatever it was worth to you."

He looked the Baron in the eye. "Whatever this trouble you're in is," he said in a somewhat harsher tone, "don't let notions of disgrace or guilt demoralise you. And keep a hold of a few quid. But don't ask me for any because I haven't got it. As I said, I'm a very very poor man these days."

He looked around the Shelbourne dining room at the businessmen who, like themselves, sat late, and had spent a good deal of their time trying to catch his eye. "Look at them," he said sotto voce. "Their demeanour is meant to suggest confidence, if not abandon. But by Jesus the afternoon thirsts suggest concealed desperations to me." He polished off his Irish coffee. "They'll survive though," he said, "most of them, if they can keep up the act." He turned his gaze on the Baron. "All right," he said seriously. "So you're in trouble. Well, do something about it. Counter attack. Don't let anything cripple you, anything, particularly the old thoughts in the long night watches. Carry on regardless with whatever it is you're supposed to be doing and make a noise about it. Are you working? How long is it since you had a ... a show ... an exhibition? You know I have a painting of your's, hanging over the fireplace in my dining room. A very beautiful ... piece. A bare tree. Reminds me of something. Somewhere I've been."

164

She twisted round a bit and then raised her arms above her head, holding for a moment the classic female pose of submission to inspection, the pose of concubine, nymph and goddess. She thought of the photographs, then of all the kinds of poses that women had to take up before men, on the stage and in those clubs and everywhere, some of them not whores at all, just girls on the stage, all the stripping and standing and pounding around like idiots, with your feet aching and your face too from the ridiculous smiling, those idiots sitting out there being the boss. And all the photographs in the English newspapers of girls on their knees with their diddies showing and their mouths open ready for it, being forced to smile at the same time. She supposed that that was how most men got their satisfaction for this cruelty thing. If you were to judge from the amount of that sort of stuff around they must all be sadists really.

She allowed that she should wear a skirt, not trousers, for the police station, but at the same time not her rather extreme new mini. The policemen would therefore miss out on whatever her legs might do for them, but never mind. Being a policeman you probably missed out on a lot anyway. Of course you probably got a bit here and there too. The blackguards probably used their power over prostitutes and delinquents in rather nasty ways.

On the way up the hill she reflected again on the Baron's duplicity. He had a bloody nerve. Well she would pay him back. She would make him hop. She smiled, a little thinly, and stretched her long athletic dancer's limbs up the hill.

The moments immediately on leaving the Minister's presence were perhaps the Baron's low. He had been deprived of his ancestry, he had no doubt about that. Both Richard Pigott's sons had died in 1915, the bad egg and the stay at home; and the dissolute old forger had no more connection with the present-day non-painter than had the man in the moon. There was only his own rather dull, rather priggish Redmondite civil-servant of a father who, admittedly, had been a friend of James Joyce and, admittedly, had been killed in the first world war. But other than him there was nothing and nobody to redeem his present state.

And his present state was terrible, there was no doubt about that either. In a way more closely relating to the Minister's kind of vitality and the Minister's kind of success, such as it was, than to that of his sculptor stepson, his sin had been brought home to him, the sin of inactivity.

He thought of his plank picture, now stashed away with the rest of his gear in the flat of a former mistress. Of course he wanted to work. He was really too old a hand to want anything else in this sorry world ... except of course money ... and perhaps respect ... and perhaps Susan. But they were all part of the same thing. Work hinged on them and they on work. It was not only the drug and the alleviation. It was also the redeemer and the source of knowledge, the revelation of order at the heart of all things, them included.

But he had no money and he was moreover going to gaol on Monday morning. He could not fucking well work when he had no money and was going to be locked up as soon as the week-end was over. How had he got himself into this position? The Minister was of course right. He was a wonder-man. Everybody else in the world had money, except himself. He thought of the company in O'Turk's. All pulling the devil by the tail of course, but all had something, while he did not even have a place to do his famous work in. He most certainly could not work in Jonathen's, that was for sure. Nor could he work in Abby's, even if she would let him stay. Besides, he was going to gaol on Monday morning. Something was going to happen on Monday morning, anyway, which would fuck him up entirely; though he had forgotten to ask what would happen when they showed up without the documents. Perhaps it was not actually on Monday that he would go to gaol.

He had a wave of feeling for his picture and its possibilities. The last and biggest of the three plank pictures, now so nearly finished. And finishable, even without the planks. Soulages, they would say, but to hell with them. He knew the difference.

He suddenly wanted to see it, to assure himself that it really existed and that he had done this thing. He wanted to see it badly, even if that meant Abby too, and although with Abby he had long reached the internal screaming and writhing stage. He paused on the corner of Merrion Street, where he had paused the day before, uncertain whether to head on towards Baggot Street, that land of discarded mistresses, or not. He found Abby almost unbearable these days, each gesture, each enthusiasm causing him intense mortification.

The heart that has truly loved, he reflected wryly. But they hadn't. Ever. It was all a cod between them. Not like ... . He thought of his lawfully wedded wife. But even when the internal screaming at every phrase or look thing sets in, desire has an odd way of returning. Desire we have always with us. And yet also nothing is more degrading than a return to a former sparring partner whose charming mannerisms afflict the sensibility. Though he had still sometimes, even recently, availed himself of her ... services.

Perhaps he might stay for a while? If stay he was allowed? He might even—Oh no, no, no, no—Susan. But Susan was out. She had made a fool of him. He would go and see his picture anyway. He had no place else to go.

"Ah! The man of the documents!"

The Baron knew the speaker, who was some sort of producer in the television and had acquired a reputation for subversive activities by blathering round the pubs. He stood now on the edge of the pavement, a leather hat at a rakish angle over one eye and his hand extended so that a finger pointed at his victim. Shocked, the Baron stared back coldly.

The speaker's companion, attired in trench coat and beret, was also known to him.

"If it isn't the man of the documents himself," said the one in the leather hat; then, evidently fearing that he had gone too far, he opened his fingers so that the outstretched hand was for shaking and added in tones of good-humoured bonhomie: "The hard man himself. Will you accompany us for a jorum? There is a little thing we would like to discuss with you."

Moved by some dreadful weakness, the Baron took the hand in apparent amity and found himself being propelled towards the door of O'Neill's.

"We hear," said the first fellow when the drinks had been ordered, "that there has been a bit of confusion about some documents."

"A bit of a mix-up," said the second.

"It is also said," said the original hailer, "that these documents may be of a somewhat incriminating nature."

"Incriminating that is," said his companion, "where certain parties who are not at this moment anxious to attract the attention of the law are concerned."

"Simply as a friend, old son, I'd like to warn you that a poor view is being taken in certain quarters," said the first one.

"Quarters whose anger is to be feared," put in the other.

"Don't ask us how we heard about this, now," said the first, putting his finger up to the side of his nose and closing one eye, "but there's a few fellows we know who are exceedingly angry about the whole thing."

"I might even go so far as to say that it would be a teeny weeny bit better to keep out of circulation for a while," affirmed the other.

"There are apparently those who believe that the mishap to the documents was no accident," said the first. "And you know what that could lead to."

"You see, we happen to be privy to certain parties' thinking about this," said the second fellow. "And we thought it would be no harm to let you know. We've known each other for a very long time, after all."

"Excuse my ignorance," said the Baron. "But what documents would these be that you are talking about?"

The first speaker raised his leather hat in mock salute. "That's rich, that is," he said.

The second one slapped the Baron on the back. "Come on now, old son. We admire your gameness. But we all know what we're talking about," he said.

"Documents of an incriminating nature," said the first, leaning forward towards the Baron, his breath redolent of tooth-rot, cigarettes and whiskey.

"That were entrusted to your keeping," said his companion.

"And have found their way into the wrong hands," said the one in the leather hat.

"Most unfortunately," said his companion.

"I hope you'll forgive me," said the Baron, "but I have to go now."

He put down his drink and left. The Baron was no masochist. Raucous laughter followed him to the door.

She crossed in front of him and bent down to pick up some typewritten sheets off the floor. The end of the black jersey parted from her jeans and bared a little stretch of ridged and indented back, the skin, though stretched, mellifluent, a golden tan.

Tan. Tanned. Bedad he often had too. Well, occasionally anyway. Laid into that fair flesh. A little lower down of course. Her plump, neat parts, where there was a nice protective layer of adipose tissue. Well, perhaps not exactly laid in. Laid in with reservations, you might say. Those reservations that spoil everything.

And it never quite got admitted between them either, if the truth were told. In fact he had known her some time before he got the hint from Ted Hughes. Why couldn't she speak out? Why couldn't he? Why couldn't everybody?

Mind you, that sort of thing could be a bit elaborate, bit ... stand-offish. And it put you under a compliment as it were, not to speak of the actual hurting.

Still, it had had, once or twice, the true intensity, the shiver down the spine that only comes from the forbidden and the dangerous.

Dangerous? Well, for her anyway. If you got carried away. If he got carried away. Ted had said that the first night, the night she had had the black belt hanging over the end of the bed, he had gone too far, larruped into her with a will, and that it hadn't made him too popular afterwards, strange to say. The Baron being a gentleman, or perhaps thinking of what Ted had told him, had never gone too far. More perhaps was the pity. But then you never knew. Never.

She got down on one knee, then the other, to reach a couple of sheets that had escaped under a chair, then swivelled round to face him, alternatively bending down on all fours and kneeling upright so that she knelt before him. Oh yes indeed, often also, he standing, she kneeling, her eyes on his, he shaken incredibly at the moment of what was to him, wrongly of course, but then the sweetness of it, her indignity. That was the true victimage, much better than any hurting. As when she knelt over him on the bed too, her breasts loose, hanging, her hair falling over him softly, her mouth working.

Her breasts were loose inside the opening of the jersey now, the skin of them whiter and smoother than the more aureate, rougher skin over neck and collarbone.

The Baron got up from his chair and stood over her, her beautiful soft dark hair also pendant as she groped on all fours again. He felt more than a little stir of impulse. This would never do. Even if. Susan.

"What's all this?" he asked. "Is this new? There seems to be a lot of it."

"Yes it's new," she answered, still on all fours. "I'm very excited about it. I really do think it's my breakthrough at last." She looked up with that slightly myopic intentness he knew. "It's a sort of long prose poem," she said. "Have you ever read the passages in "Contre Sainte Beuve" about the romantic fulfillment that seems to be promised by the faces of complete strangers? The passages that really started Proust off? That contain the germ of "A La Recherche"? Well, I think they've started me off too."

She smiled, that crooked, thin-lipped, shy smile that had perhaps started the Baron off; once upon a time. And her eyes were beautiful too, brown and uncertain. But he bitterly regretted having asked. He might have to read something, and, worse, to enthuse over it.

"I'd adore you to read it," she said. "It's very visual I think. A new thing for me." She stood up, straightened up, pushed back her hair, and, with papers in hand, pulled down her jersey, an action which stretched the fabric from breasts to waist. He observed her nipples, which showed briefly till the fabric relaxed again, and admired as always the declension to hips. At least all the women he had ever had anything to do with had been, in the common sense, highly desirable. But then too they had always been artists or artistes, and therefore, sooner or later, ravening egotists. His lawfully wedded wife for

170

example was a writer, a publishing and publishable writer (which was more than could be said for Abby), and an autobiographical writer to boot, a sensitive autobiographer, which compounded all the offences. He was in two books thinly disguised, and he would never, ever forgive. He would get himself a girl, an Irish girl, convent educated by the Dominicans or the Sisters of the Sacred Heart, with no artistic or creative ambitions, and she would minister to his needs. Susan? But Susan wasn't. She had been on the stage.

"I can't read it now I'm afraid."

"I suppose you'd like a drink?" she said, not altogether kindly and with a small wry embitterment of that thin-lipped, shy smile.

"I'm not altogether pushed," he answered, a little more harshly and awkwardly than he intended.

"I've only got Scotch," she said, "and not much of that."

"You were never one for unnecessary apologies before," said the Baron. "Why start now?"

There was a certain loss of composure, he thought, in the way she put down the papers and walked out, as if she was oddly conscious of his regard.

He had been here last on the day he first heard the news of prosecution, disgrace and calamity. Drunk.

When she came back, though with a decent enough drink, she was, he saw from the corners of her mouth, about to be cruel. Well God blast it, no, He would not put up with her tongue. He had stood enough today. He put out a hand, she thought for the whiskey, and put the glass in it.

"What will you do?" she asked.

"What do you mean do," he countered.

"Well you can't go on like this."

"Like what?"

"Well, you're not doing any work. It's disgraceful. I mean it's wrong. It's terrible. That painting I've got. That's the one you were working on months ago. And now I hear you're in some sort of awful mess or other."

The Baron sipped his drink. He felt the disadvantage of his

position and his own bodily awkwardness. She looked down at him with a terrible intensity. Her face looked older in aggression, like all faces. He was in for an hour or so of steady suffering, of being made to see himself, such as he was these days, through hostile and malevolent eyes, of being damaged irreparably maybe, for no reason at all that he could think of, since he could always go, but he wouldn't go, he knew that. He was, he must be, a masochist to stay.

"You see, my dear friend," the Lecturer was saying to Riley as the Baron came into O'Turk's, "at our age one has had time to reflect on the destructions and deteriorations of personality which are an inevitable consequence of romantic and emotional unions, of all unions other than the most—if I may put it that way—impersonal ones."

They were seated just inside the back door. Someone else, who was invisible because of a raised *Sporting Chronicle,* was at the next table. From behind the journal came a curious hawking noise. In some trepidation because of the person at the next table the Baron sat down.

"The damage," continued the Lecturer as he did so, "that the parties mutually do to the only thing which matters in either of them, the sacred, mysterious, godgiven, human personality, is too appalling for a moral man to contemplate, particularly, if I may say so, in the case where one or other has a creative personality. If one cannot do without bodily sexual conjunction one should confine oneself to those transient encounters in which the other party is a mere accomplice or convenience. If these cannot be safely and hygienically arranged one should consider the advantages of those types of visual concurrence to which modern metropolitan man everywhere is becoming more and more addicted, which indeed he seems to think more pleasurable and, on the whole, more satisfactory."

"Not in the island of saints and scholars," said a voice from behind the *Sporting Chronicle.*

"We are not entirely cut off from the outside world," countered the Lecturer somewhat testily, apparently not

172

pleased at the interruption.

"Ireland is an island entirely surrounded by water," said the voice.

"There are such things as aeroplanes," replied the Lecturer.

"And dangerous, unreliable yokes they are, too," said Riley.

"Pray do not be flippant, Patrick, and pray refrain from joining in these interruptions," said the Lecturer. "As I was saying, given the pleasures, freedoms and choices provided by the alternatives, knowing the dangers, the drawbacks, the unhappy discoveries and unfoldings, the deceits and disillusionments that inevitably, as we have seen, attend any form of prolonged or pretended emotional involvement, to say nothing of the responsibilities, equally dismaying and corrupting whether shouldered or unshouldered, what man of honour, what philosopher even, but must prefer them, particularly when he takes a retrospective view of his previous errors and crimes."

"He has a point there by God," said the voice. "And it's a moral one."

"But what about the pleasures of pursuit and conquest?" asked Riley.

"Yes," said the Baron somewhat bitterly. "Hours spent chasing after something which ought to be brought up to the back door every morning with the milk."

"When compared with the effortless dominance over an entire sex provided by commerce in our society, the forms of domination gladly submitted to, whether for monetary or other reasons, and the almost unlimited humiliations willingly suffered by the countless thousands who allow themselves to be exhibited in dress and undress, and whether in reality or through photographic representation, individual conquest scarcely seems to me to be a psychological necessity," said the Lecturer sternly.

"Right again," said the voice. "Since the camera came in every second woman in the world was turned out to be a whore. And the richer they are the more they will do for notice."

During the mystified silence which followed this last

173

remark the lecturer gathered his papers and his gaberdine together and swept out in the manner of a practised audience leaver.

Riley turned to the Baron. "That girl of yours," he said. "She wants you to meet her at five o'clock."

"She what?" asked the Baron in some astonishment.

Riley shot a warning glance at the next table. "She wants you to meet her in Dun Laoghaire at five o'clock," he went on, lowering his voice. "She suggested a pub called Ganavan's. She wondered whether you would know it. I assured her you did. It's only a little after four now, so why not take her up on it?"

The Baron glanced over at the clock. It was indeed after four. Then he looked back at his friend.

"But how did you get the message?" he asked. "Where did you meet her?"

"She rang me up," said Riley.

"From where?" asked the Baron, still puzzled. He stole a look at the *Sporting Chronicle,* now bearing the aspect of a scanning and listening apparatus. "From the office or from out there?" he asked.

"Oh, from out there," said Riley amiably. "I rather gathered she didn't go to the office at all today. And if I were you it's out there I'd go too. It seems to me she has something to tell you. Whether it's germane to your major concerns or not I do not know, but in any case it's always a good thing to meet girls near to where they live. More particularly when they have the house to themselves."

The Baron stood up to go. Then something else occurred to him.

"How did she get your telephone number?" he asked.

"Oh, I gave it to her last night," said Riley blandly. "But it's time for you to go. It really is."

"O time be merciful in your disclosures," said the voice from behind the racing paper.

"That was thoughtful of you," said the Baron, and went.

She was sitting under the oleograph of the gallant Munsters. Confused and nervous though he was, the Baron registered that she was wearing a yellow, flower-patterned sleeveless, summer dress, rather longer than that of last night, but revealing her beautiful knees. It had a leather belt at the waist. Her suede jacket was on the seat beside her and her bare arms were beautiful too. She looked remarkably cool and composed.

"Did you know this place?" she asked.

He nodded, playing for time.

"I somehow thought you would," she said.

She pressed the bell and an apprentice pulled back the shutter of the hatch. At least he was spared Mr Ganavan.

"Have a drink," she said.

"Well, I will, actually," said the Baron.

"Of course you will," she said. "What sort?"

"A Scotch," said the Baron. "It's what I usually have at this time of day," he added foolishly.

"A Scotch for Mr Ponsonby," said Susan. "Or is it Pigott? Or Power?"

"Pigott will do," he said.

"Just so long as we know," said Susan.

"Better make it a large one," she added to the waiting lad. "Mr Pigott probably needs it."

"Why don't you sit down," she said, patting the seat beside her. "You look silly standing there like that."

He did as he was told. She was disturbingly close and beautiful.

The apprentice placed the drink on the ledge, accompanying it with a small jug of water. Susan placed them both in front of the Baron—considerately, you might even say, he thought—and then, as he mixed, she proceeded to pay. The business accomplished, she turned to face him. She was wearing make-up. He could see the lovely skin serrations under her lipstick. She was, he thought, rather carefully made-up.

"I was going to play a game with you," she said, "but there's something you ought to know straight away."

He waited, his heart beating, his emotions a mixture of anxiety, affection and desire.

"Those people," she said, "—your guardians—your uncle

175

and aunt or whatever they were. They're dead."

"Good God," said the Baron. He couldn't think of anything else to say.

"They were killed in a coach crash in England," she said; and added: "At Stratford-on-Avon, of all places. The Guards' came round to tell me this morning."

"Good God," he said again; and immediately thought of his box and his papers; but even in this crisis some part of his mind registered that that "at Stratford-on-Avon, of all places" suggested more general intelligence and sophistication than he was still giving her credit for.

"They were your uncle and aunt?" she asked.

The Baron nodded. As the old stories have it, he couldn't trust himself to do more.

"Well you're a strange fellow," she said. "There's no mistake about that. I don't suppose you're grief-stricken."

"I scarcely knew them," he said.

"They brought you up," she said.

"It makes no odds," he said. "I scarcely knew them."

"I wonder," Susan said, considering him.

"What about my box?" he said, straight out.

"If you mean the box you were asking me about when you were telling me all those lies," she began, and then broke off to ask: "Do you mean the box you were giving me those ridiculous reasons for wanting?"

The Baron nodded. "Well, where is it?" he asked.

"How should I know? It's not there anyway," she replied; and then, as if taking pity on him, she added: "But there is some stuff in the house that might interest you."

She began to stand up. "You'd better come and see," she said. "In any case I've got a few things that I certainly want to ask you about myself."

They went into the house by the front door, to which Susan had a key; and then into the front room where the Baron's last interview with his guardians had taken place. He felt at once the hostility of the icons. Wherever I belonged, he thought, it wasn't here. But bare-armed Susan in her summer frock was a foreign presence among these signs and emblems too, whether hostile to him also or not.

Coming down the road between the dogs he had scarcely risked a word, and to those he had risked she had answered only with considering looks. And yet also, coming down the road, some sort of pleasure in her mere proximity had begun to prevail over his various anxieties.

He decided to take the naggin of whiskey he had secretly bought before leaving the pub out of his pocket. "I think I'll have a drink," he said.

Susan regarded this action quizzically also. "You drink too much, you know. You really do," she said. Then, rather surprisingly, she added. "Perhaps we'd both better have a drink."

She bent to open a glass-fronted cabinet and took out two glasses. "Hold on a minute," she said, "I'll get some water."

When she came back with a glass jug the Baron was seated rather miserably in one of the armchairs which, with an equally solid and forbidding sofa, composed a suite of three pieces. Susan sat down in the other and took it upon herself to pour the drinks. Then she settled coolly back in the chair, kicked off her shoes and brought her lovely feet up from the floor.

"Maybe it's none of my business," she said. "But I would like to hear the whole story."

The Baron had the same impulse to tell her all, whatever the consequences, that he had had the night before in Doheny and Nesbitt's. "You mean from the beginning?" he asked. "Right from the beginning?"

"Yes, of course from the beginning," she said. "I want to know all about it. I'm an interested party."

And so he told her: right from the beginning, sitting there in that horrible room among the momentoes of things past, just as he had told Riley the day before.

Susan interrupted occasionally to ask questions, but they weren't always the sort he might have expected.

"This town you were brought up in," she asked, shortly after he had begun—"Did you have any friends there?"

"None," he answered. "My uncle was unpopular for some reason, I don't know why. Perhaps because he was an interloper of some sort. Anyway my school fellows had some sort of a set against me. They stoned me once or twice on our way to school."

He paused. Susan was looking at him intently. He felt he had to add something. "Like his schoolfellows did to Trollope on the way to Harrow," he added.

"Yes, well I don't know anything about that," said Susan. "There's a lot I don't know. And in any case it's you I want to hear about."

And so he went on, his confidence increasing as he did. Susan asked about his aunt and his relationship with her, which he said was non-existent. When he got to the bit about the reason for the strike she said, "Well I think you might have made some sort of a protest about the poor girl that was involved, the skivvy or whatever you called her." At a later point in his story she picked up some small clue and, somewhat to his distress, asked about his marriage.

Otherwise she was silent. When he came towards the end she said:

"So that's what you were after. You had no interest in me at all."

"Oh no, no," the Baron said miserably. "I think you're very ... attractive. Very ... beautiful. I mean I think you're a nice person and I wanted to ... get to know you better." Then he saw how she was looking at him. "I still do," he added. Susan said nothing. "A lot better," he said, hoping not to appear completely idiotic, but it sounded merely arch.

When he was altogether finished, she said:

"I suppose it never occurred to you that you could have saved yourself a lot of trouble simply by telling me who you were in the first place? Maybe I'd have let you have your precious box if you'd simply asked me straight out. I wonder would I? Anyway you'll never know now, will you?"

"You're sure it's not here?" he asked desperately.

She nodded. "Quite sure," she said. "On the other hand now that I've heard the story ... ." She stopped and smiled secretively. "But first things first," she said. "Wait there."

She got up from her chair and went out of the room leaving her shoes behind. When she came back she handed him a piece of newspaper. It was a photograph, neatly clipped out and marked, in his aunt's handwriting, "Dubliner's Diary, Evening

178

Press, January 1962". The caption underneath said: "The artist Ronald Ponsonby with the Minister for Justice Mr J. J. Fogarty at an exhibition of the former's paintings which was opened by the Minister at the Hibernian Galleries last night."

The Baron handed it back. "That exhibition was a flop," he said, "A complete and utter flop. There were only three pictures sold. His nibs bought one of them. A tree piece. It reminded him of something."

Susan said nothing. She was still standing beside him in her stockinged feet.

"I suppose that's how you knew I was connected with them," he added lamely.

"She kept that," Susan said. "And she kept a lot of other things too. You never gave her a chance, did you? I wonder why? You never trusted her."

She went to where her high-heeled shoes were and inserted her beautiful feet into them.

"You probably don't trust women very much," she said. "Maybe you don't even like them." Then she crossed to the door. "I've got something to show you upstairs," she said. "Come on."

The steps up to the attic had proved yesterday to be surprisingly like the steps he had remembered from the house in Ballywhidder, but the place itself had seemed larger and barer. Now it seemed smaller again. More or less the same size. And very like. There was a bed with a bare mattress which, for some reason, preoccupied though he was supposed to be with other matters, the Baron now found disturbing. He had a sudden impulse to pull her down on it and put this whole matter on a proper basis.

"I suppose this is where the slavey slept in the old days," she said coolly. "Was there a slavey in the attic in Ballywhidder?"

He nodded. "Funny you were able to spend all that time up there, then," she said. It was too, but he couldn't remember how that had come about. He couldn't remember any feeling about the attic as being occupied. He mustn't have thought of the maids as human beings somehow.

Under the sloping roof was the junk he remembered from yesterday. He knew his box was not amongst it but Susan now pointed to an ordinary cardboard box which was in a corner under the rafters.

"The stuff is in there," she said pointing to it. "All that stuff you were talking about, the letters and bills and photographs and things. It's all in there. I wasn't lying when I said I didn't know where your box had gone. They did something with it. But before that they moved the stuff out of it and put it all in there."

The Baron got down on his knees, his heart thumping, and lifted up the cardboard flaps of the box. There, right enough, were the newspapers.

He lifted them out carefully and put them on the floor. There was an old basket-work armchair under the roof also. Susan pulled it towards her and sat down. "They got rid of the other box for some reason and put the stuff in this," she said. "I realised that when you told me the story."

She picked up a copy of *The Flag of Ireland.*

"Was your grandfather connected with these?" she asked.

The Baron began to give her a sort of history lesson. Then he came to the sheet of brown paper which, just as it had done before, separated the first layer from the next. The next was the photographs.

"Have you looked at these?" he asked, handing her one.

"Yes," said Susan. "I sort of dug into the box earlier today. I got this far."

He found himself handing them to her one by one, he did not quite know why. After about four he stole a look at her face. She was apparently absorbed in what she was looking at and did not seem to notice. He handed her another.

"They're not for real, are they?" Susan asked. "I mean it's only acting, isn't it?"

"Oh these were staged, I should think," said the Baron; but he was going to tell her about Lyons and all the rest of it when she went on.

"In that case," she said, "whoever thought these were a big deal was easily pleased. I mean if they knew it was a cod ... ."

"Oh, I don't think that necessarily follows," said the Baron, a tiny bit peeved. "It doesn't always work like that with people. And anyway," he added, "at the very least they knew the girls had had to strip off and let themselves be tied up while the photographs were taken. At a time when most women were very shy about revealing themselves the thought that somebody had had to do that—even for money—might have been enough."

"Maybe the bitches were enjoying themselves though," said Susan. "It might be a bit of a thrill to pretend at it, all stripped off and everything." Well I never, the Baron thought, but she went on hurriedly: "They'd be enjoying the teasing anyway, some of them. Lots of girls do, particularly when it's photographs."

But of course she had been on the stage the Baron reflected. Maybe somebody had taken a few photographs of her in various ... poses. He looked at her again. She put the photographs she was holding carefully down on the brown paper which had covered them and then put her hair back with both hands.

"I'm not going to read the books, if that's what you're thinking," she said. "Life's too short."

The Baron hurried on to the next layer, telling her some more about Pigott while he went through the bills. When they came to the red leather writing case whose lock he had forced so long ago he noted that there was no need to tell her anything about Parnell. She seemed to know the story. But then they had already discussed it. A few moments later he noticed that she seemed to know quite a bit about Joyce too. And he was in two minds about literacy in women. At least before he took them in hand.

When they got to the things at the end—the woman's chemise, the child's bonnet with strings, the Rubaiyat of Omar Khayyam with the crushed rose inside it—she held them all briefly for a moment or so in her hands before putting them down too on the corner of the sheet of paper; and she read one or two of the Baron's mother's letters to his father with a furrowed brow.

"Your mother's name was definitely Philomena?" she asked then.

The Baron nodded.

"And your father's name was definitely Richard Power?"

"Yes."

"And those letters from Joyce and who-not are to him anyway—I mean they are to your father no matter what we believe about his ancestry. Right?"

The Baron nodded. "Right," he said. It was right.

"But you still don't know how this stuff—all this stuff relating to Richard Pigott would have got into your father's hands?"

The Baron shook his head.

"Bit of a mystery there, then, apart from anything else, isn't there? I mean if there had been a name change and a suppression of identity and all that?"

The Baron nodded. There was a bit of a mystery there, apart from anything else.

After a while the Baron said: "Well, I suppose we'd better put this stuff back." And he was about to put it back, layer by layer, when Susan said, "What's this then?" and handed him an envelope which had been lying at the bottom of the box.

The Baron turned it over in his hands. It was an expensive, bluish envelope and on the front was written: "To my sons and grandsons." The handwriting was what is called copper-plate and there was a flourish underneath. The Baron's heart began to thump.

"Is that Pigott's writing?" asked Susan.

The Baron was struck by a thought. "Do you know," he said, "I've never actually seen Pigott's writing. There was nothing in his writing in the box."

"Well open it," said Susan. "You're supposed to be his grandson."

It opened easily because the flap wasn't stuck down. Inside was a solitary sheet of paper, of the same bluish colour and with writing in the same hand. It was numbered 3 at the top as if there had been other sheets; and the 3 had a flourish under it also. With Susan listening, the Baron read it out. It seemed to him familiar, but he couldn't say from where. "One more word," it said, "about disgrace. The word has nothing to do with a man's actions. It has to do with the favour of his fellows, who choose to look upon him either as a blackguard or an omadhaun or both. But these reactions are usually imagined by the disgraced party and one of the reasons they lock you away in gaol is to force you to imagine them. The same applies to making you resign if you don't mind from your clubs. But as a matter of fact I have never seen anybody eating his chop alone as a result of any crime or series of crimes, or idiocy or series of idiocies whatever, provided he was mildly amusing and had a few quid for food and drink. Personal unpleasantness is another matter and is often the result of demoralisation. So don't let notions of disgrace or guilt demoralise you. And keep a hold of a few quid."

"Well that doesn't get us very far," said Susan after a pause.

"No," said the Baron. "I'm afraid that's not much good to man or beast." But where had he seen it before?

"If you ask me it's about time you started to believe whatever you want to believe," said Susan. "I mean believe whatever you want to believe and give up worrying about it. As far as I'm concerned you can be the great Richard Pigott's grandson if you want, O.K.?"

The Baron nodded his head. He threw the envelope back into the bottom of the box. It was O.K.

"All right then", said Susan. "Maybe it's a pity that there isn't something here which would prove whatever it is you want proved, but earlier today I discovered something that I think is a damn sight more important. Come on and I'll show you."

She led the way down the bare wooden stairs from the attic again; and then all the way down to the kitchen where earlier that day she had sat with the police.

"Sit down there," she said, pointing to a chair at the decent, well scrubbed, plain deal table. The Baron did as he was told.

Susan went to the dresser, on the ledge of which there was a small pile of papers. After some hesitation she took out a long manila envelope and then returned to the table and sat down.

"Did you know that I am an orphan too?" she asked looking the Baron directly in the eye.

He shook his head.

"Well I am," she said. "And it turns out that we orphans of the storm have been the cause of a great deal of concern to our aunt and our uncle—if I may call them so. Although of course

183

they were much more your aunt and uncle than they were mine. I'm once removed or something. However, that's not the point. The point is that they appear to have made three wills and that copies of all three of them are here in this house."

She picked up the envelope and held it between a well-made thumb and finger, smiling peculiarly as she did so.

"The first will leaves everything to you," she said. "Everything we die possessed of to our dearly beloved nephew Richard Power," just like that, bingo bango. It's dated 1938. Richard Power is your name, isn't it?"

"Yes, but ... Well, it was," said the Baron. "But ... ."

"Before you say anything let me tell you that everything we die possessed of, or everything they actually did die possessed of, appears to be a lot. There are bank statements here too, and it's ten thousand or so anyway, not to mention the mansion we're in, which they owned, and which at today's prices must be worth another ten thousand at least. But that isn't the whole story."

She put the documents she had been holding down on the table, went to the dresser again and returned with another. "It never is," said the Baron, in response to her last remark, and even as he admired her straight back.

Susan sat down again, smoothing her skirt underneath her with one hand. In the other hand she held a second envelope. "Unfortunately for you," she said, "there is a second will. It's dated a year ago, which was shortly after I came to stay, and it leaves everything to me."

"You were here a year ago?" asked the Baron foolishly. "You were here ... all the time?"

"Indeed then and I was," she said smiling. "We must have just missed each other once or twice. But that's neither here nor there. Are you disappointed about everything being left to me?"

The Baron nodded, as glumly as he could considering she was smiling at him. He supposed he was.

"Well, I won't spin it out any longer," she said. "The fact is that there's another one, a third, and, strange as it may seem, it leaves everything to us both. 'Jointly', it says. Here, I'll get it."

She went to the dresser again, thus giving the Baron

another rear view, and this time when she came back she handed him a third document which she had already taken from its envelope. Though he by no means had his wits about him, the Baron made shift to read it. Indeed he read it aloud.

"To our niece, Susan Blackshaw," he read, "the daughter of our sister Edna's late son, Martin ... and to our nephew and adopted son Richard, provided that he acknowledges his real name."

He put the paper down on the table. "What sort of a carry-on is this?" he asked bitterly, "foxing a fellow, muddling him up all his life and then making a clown out of him by offering him money to deny his own ... ."

He stopped, words apparently having failed him.

"Identity?" suggested Susan.

"That's right," he said, "identity. I won't do it. They can stuff their house and their money."

"But maybe you have already satisfied the condition," Susan said. "Maybe you have acknowledged your real name."

"No," said the Baron. "That's not what they mean. They want me to go back to my ... original name. And I won't do it."

"In which case I get the whole lot," said Susan.

"I don't mind," said the Baron. "You're heartily welcome as far as I'm concerned."

"I'll be a quite rich girl."

"Glad to make your acquaintance."

"Yes. I suppose you'll start making up to me now just because I'm an unprotected orphan with a few quid."

"I'm an orphan myself."

"All right then. Let's assume you have already acknowledged your real name and split it."

"What?"

"Let's just do what I said. Split it."

"If there was a row about it," said the Baron, "I mean if you wanted to contest the thing, you'd probably get the lot no matter what I did."

"It would make a nice law case," said Susan. "And of course it would be great fun for you trying to prove you were Pigott."

"I don't want any part of it. You can have it all."

"You'll have to offer them their money back on Monday morning as well as the papers if you're going to stay out of gaol. As things stand you haven't got any money and you don't even own the stuff that was in the box."

"Well of all the bloody bitches ... ."

"Cool down. If we split you can have the stuff in the box and we'd probably be able to go straight to the bank and get some money. You don't really want to go to gaol do you?"

"I don't care whether I do or not."

Susan leaned across the table and took his face in her hands. Then she ran her fingers through his tangled grey hair.

"Well then," she said. "That's that. Normally speaking, in the case of someone I liked as much as I do you, I would be hoping that the proceedings would end in a good fuck, but I don't fuck with fellows when I know it's only going to be once off. Right or wrong it doesn't seem to suit me, so if you're going to go to gaol on Monday morning I don't want to get myself muddled up. Of course there's always the chance that people won't make out and that it will only be the one time anyway, I suppose, but that's different; and actually I find that if you like somebody fucking hardly ever puts you off them, so you can have a few more tries. But this way it's no go."

The Baron found himself quite breathless.

"O.K.," he said. "I'll take whatever's necessary to stay out of gaol."

"Half of everything or nothing at all," said Susan.

"Oh all right then," said the Baron.

She smiled at him, a little nervously he thought.

"Well that's the end of the first part of the proceedings then," she said. "What about the second?"

"Let's go for a drink first," said the Baron. "I really do need one."

Susan laughed. She seemed relieved. "I knew you'd say that," she said.

In the pub the Baron said: "There are a couple of things puzzling me. Where did the stuff in England come from?"

"I've been thinking about that," said Susan, "and your man

186

in the Celtic Library—the Gaeiligoir bollocks or whatever you call him—seems to be the guilty party. He must have hived off some of the stuff and sold it to this dealer fellow. On his own account I mean. After all the library had no list of what you gave him, did it?"

The Baron shook his head. "Not so far as I know it wouldn't have," he said.

"Well it might be possible that when he began to have doubts first he saw this ad in "Hibernia", decided to try if the stuff would pass this dealer—to assure himself that it would also convince anybody else who looked at it—was tempted and fell. Does he have any need of money? Does he read "Hibernia"?"

The Baron looked at her sharply. "All these fellows need money," he said. "The only way they can get women is to wine them and dine them.They're always wining and dining their secretaries and students and suchlike."

"Well, there you are then," said Susan. "Putting the law on you afterwards may only have been some sort of cover-up for that. But equally selling some of the stuff to the dealer may have been an attempt to cover up the blunder he had made by buying it in the first place. He might have hoped to give it all some sort of authentication by having reputable dealers hawking some of it round. Personally, though, I favour the theory that he did it for gain. Because of the wining and dining," she added, smiling at him.

"Of course he was going off his rocker," said the Baron, "so there's no knowing now what may have been in or on his mind."

"I wouldn't pay too much attention to that," said Susan. "Lots of people go into these places when things get too tough for them. Particularly fellows who are in good jobs like that and know they are going to be looked after."

The Baron gazed at her again in admiration. She was as intelligent as all get out. But she showed little sign of neurotic disorder. In his experience intelligent people, intelligent women especially, tended to be highly neurotic, and he was accustomed to look for signs of incipient neurosis in the women he took up with, especially the intelligent ones, as

187

travellers in the middle-ages had looked for signs of leprosy of bubonic plague. But he could discern none in this girl.

"And the long nights I've thought of him," he said, "when the rain was on the roof. What really bothered me was not the fear of the gaol and the jeers but the damage I thought I had done to him. Him and his wife. The real, unadulterated remorse."

"What's the wife got to do with it?" asked Susan.

"Oh nothing," said the Baron hastily. "Just that I thought she must have suffered a bit too. On account of him going off his rocker I mean."

A little later on he said: "Another thing. What about that note that Johnny Fogarty saw in the file? R.P. died such and such a date in 1915? Wouldn't that seem to rule me out?"

Susan looked at him tenderly. "Don't you see?" she asked. "He made the entry himself. He was off to the war. It was the end of his old life. There was a widespread feeling then that going off to the war was a sort of re-birth."

The Baron gazed back at her. Was she too intelligent? One way or another they were already sort of friends. Not to say fellow conspirators. And co-tenants of a house. He had to press some sort of switch in his mind to make her again a mere object of desire.

Some invoke the imagination and its almost absolute powers to give them a choice of the circumstances in which sexual converse takes place, and to alter if needs be the other party's role, status, character and psychological disposition. Thus they choose that they should only be suffered to do by threat or compulsion what is in fact freely allowed, or they choose that what is in reality gladly permitted should only have been attained to because the other party was bound by some form of constraint or contract, being a prisoner in a South American brothel, an innocent in an Arabian harem, a bought Victorian bride, a virtuous heroine yielding to save her lover from an awful fate, a starlet on the casting couch, an Irish servant in Boston, a teenager hoping for more dates, a dancer trying to make the chorus line, a career girl on the make.

In this way they create, where none exists, a semblance of victimage; and put the companion of the hour in any one of the multitude of predicaments in which women have found themselves over the ages, perhaps in more than one at a time. To do this, and to fit the other party's responses into the rough outlines of the scenario, requires of course a modicum of imaginative ingenuity, but not as much as one might think, for even a genuine response can be interpreted as desperately faked, perhaps even in an extreme state of mental and bodily discomfort, or while suffering agonies of disgust; and in any case the manifestations and signs of female ecstasy resemble very closely those of torment and distress.

So much for the idea that all males demand the true signs and portents of delight from the female. Many do. Some do not. Or not always. Or not at certain points of the proceedings.

The Baron thought there was something missing from sexual conjunction, though, if, sooner or later, the other person did not get as much out of it, in her own way, as he did in his. His own enjoyment secured in fact or in prospect, the idea of the girl enjoying herself too was even a source of excitement to him. He suffered for her, as you might say, until she came, whether as a result of the caressing, which he delighted to prolong, or of the act itself; and with Susan, whose satisfaction in both cases was evident (though just possibly, in the second case, the Baron was inclined to suspect, with her as with others, a well-meaning fake, about the necessity for which it might be possible soon to talk) he certainly did not feel tempted to mingle any fantasy with any part of the occasion, the fact being that from the beginning, as her clothes came off, he had continued to feel for this long-legged girl who was his friend a happy tenderness of a sort which did not by any means inhibit his pleasure and eventually became even part of it.

So his heart sang now as she sat up in bed with his jacket over her thin shoulders, sipping whiskey, her breasts loose, looked at him out of those full, bright, brown eyes, frowned a girl's frown and asked:

"What was he like, this grandfather of yours? I mean what

was he really like?"

"Well the words his contemporaries applied to him were slimy, oily, snake-like."

"That was after he was found out?"

"Oh, of course after he was found out. Before that a lot of people seemed to find him quite charming."

"And what do you think of him?"

"Oh, I suppose he was all right. He really did go to the shabbiest lengths to get money."

"Perhaps the poor man needed it."

"It depends on what you call need. I suppose it took quite a lot of money to have the sort of fun he wanted in the sort of brothels he went to. The wear and tear on the girls would be considerable."

Susan seemed a little taken aback. "H'mm", she said. "So that was what he wanted, was it?"

"Of course it was. You've seen the pictures. I rather fancy he couldn't have enough of it."

"And would you have taken after him by any chance? You're not a sadist yourself I suppose?"

"Stick around," said the Baron grimly. He pinched her thigh. "Stick around for a while and you'll find out," he said.

"I don't think you're a sadist," Susan said, pinching him back. Hard. So that it really did hurt. "You're far too rough. Sadists are kind of afraid of women. I know because I met one once and he was terrified."

"I'll have you know," said the Baron, sitting straight up and beginning at last to lecture in his turn, "that sexual sadists are a much maligned and misunderstood lot. Indeed the word sadist is a much misused and misunderstood word. Those dull clots, Hitler and Stalin are supposed to have been sadists, but there is absolutely no evidence that either of them were sadists in the sexual sense at all, or had any leanings whatsoever in that direction. In fact one of the strangest things about the whole appalling history of political tyranny in our time is how small a part truly sexual sadism appears to have played in it. The people who ran the camps, the bosses and the guards, had, you might think, unlimited opportunities to indulge their sadistic sexual tendencies if they'd had any, but in fact overt

190

sexual sadism was as rare as the flowers in May. Most of the sadism, if that is what you like to call it, was bureaucratic, and took place at a distance from the all too readily available flesh. In spite of the almost unlimited opportunities there were for that sort of gratification, so few of the prime movers or even the immediate bullies in the concentration camps and prisons, east and west, showed themselves to be sexual sadists in the proper sense that one is forced to conclude that sexual sadists are not attracted to that sort of situation, any more than they are moved to be dentists or judges or knife-throwers."

"Golly," said Susan.

"It may even be the case," said the Baron somewhat heatedly, "that true sexual sadists are among the most considerate and amicable of people. Many of them are, as you correctly point out, afraid of the opposite sex. In the ordinary course of events most of them would, it is fairly safe to say, be reluctant to hurt a fly. And observation has shown that even those of them who can not be convicted of timidity are likely to be the soul of courtesy and kindness in their ordinary, run of the mill dealings with women."

"But of course," said Susan. "Except when they're hanging them from the ceiling by the wrists, or laying into them with whips."

"I mean in their relationships otherwise," said the Baron. "Sadists are not, as is commonly supposed, bullies. Neither are they monsters who rejoice in the sight of blood. They are rarely killers or psychopaths. They do not always seek to inflict mental or other suffering on those they associate with. They do not necessarily enjoy pain."

"Imagine that now," said Susan, "they must be nice fellows."

"It is also a mistake to believe," said the Baron, "that most sadists go prowling around on dark nights looking for unwilling victims. Most sadists are reasonable people and they know that the laws of supply and demand apply to sadism just as much as to anything else. I agree that my grandfather availed himself of unwilling victims and that that is a black mark against him, but there is no proof that he was typical and I certainly don't pretend that he was admirable."

"Oh well," Susan said, "maybe he was unlucky. I'm sure there are girls who like that sort of thing. Maybe he just never met them. Or maybe he just didn't know. You never do know with anybody till you try, do you? It might even be a case of 'nobody asked me, sir'," she said.

She leaned down and gave him a quick kiss; and then, slipping off her jacket, turned delicate shoulder blades and indented backbone towards him as she bent over and put her glass on the floor.

"That's exactly what I mean," said the Baron, eyeing her naked back. "It's a question of getting suited." He said nothing about the ability of the imagination to create illusions of dominance and submission. It was, he thought, scarcely worth mentioning.

She twisted round towards him again, slid down in the bed and put her hand on his hip, her head on the pillow.

"Did he have any friends?" she asked.

"Well there was Lord Muskerry and people like that. The membership of the Royal St George Yacht Club, if you call them friends. He probably did."

"What about women friends?"

"I don't know," said the Baron. "I don't know of any relationship with women except of the kind we've been talking about."

"No wonder he went to the dogs," said Susan. "Still he must have had something to recommend him if he was an ancestor of yours. He can't have been all bad."

"I suppose what he really was," said the Baron, "was a boulevardier who liked to swagger along with a flower in his buttonhole and who hated certain forms of unpleasantness—certain only, mind you, he was quite blind to the ones he did engage in—so desperately that they caught up with him in the end and destroyed him, as the things we hate mostly do." He paused for a moment. What was it the Minister had said?

"An elite spirit who felt he should be free in some way from the degrading conditions under which most lives are lived," he said.

"H'mm," Susan said. "I suppose you could say it's not a

bad formula. It's not right for an artist, though, is it?"

"What do you mean?"

"Well, I always thought artists were more down to earth sort of people. I suppose with all this stuff about your ancestry and history and all the rest of it you were trying to turn yourself into some sort of aristocrat so you could be above the herd too. And it won't wash. It's about time you gave it up."

"I suppose it is," said the Baron.

"You see that's what this aristocracy lark is about—wanting to be free from the conditions under which ordinary lives are lived—and I might be wrong but I don't see that as the artist's bag at all," said Susan.

"I suppose you're right," said the Baron.

"Besides which," she said, "it could just be that ... ." She looked up at him out of the corner of one brown eye. "Those letters from James Joyce," she said. " "They are in his handwriting I suppose?"

The Baron nodded. "I've checked," he said.

"And the Parnell letters?"

"I've checked on his writing too," the Baron said. "There's no doubt about it. They're his all right."

"Unless somebody forged them," Susan said.

The thought had not occurred to the Baron. "Oh no," he said. "Surely not. That would be preposterous. Besides which, who would want to do it?"

"Pigott," said Susan softly.

"Well, even if Pigott forged Parnell's, what about the Joyce letters? Who would want to forge them?"

"Maybe somebody forged the whole lot," Susan said.

"That's preposterous," said the Baron. "I can't think why anybody would want to do that."

"Well," she murmured. "You forged the whole lot, didn't you?"

He looked down to see if she was joking, but her eyes were closed and she was already almost asleep, so he lay down himself and put his arms round her, amazed as always by the softness and vulnerability of the female flesh. After a while he began to think of the work he could now do and of the fun and comradeship, never mind anything else, they would enjoy

193

betimes. That house in the garden, he reflected, the one he had burgled the day before, would make an admirable studio, and he now had money enough to go on working for ever and a day. But he couldn't get that last suggestion of hers out of his head either.